A voice from her past . . .

"So you have time to talk?" Claire asked. "I heard some great gossip today. About Ashley Franklin and Gary Wilson."

Jenny chuckled. "Spill."

She and Claire talked and gossiped for nearly half an hour. The relaxed conversation made Jenny feel good.

I'm back to normal, she thought. Back to a normal life. Back to myself again.

Then, a few minutes later, the phone rang again.

And Jenny heard the voice she hoped never to hear again.

The whispered, raspy voice that had filled her life with so much horror.

"Hi, Jenny," he whispered. *"Hi, Jenny — it's me."*

Don't miss these other thrillers
by R.L. Stine:

The BABYSITTER IV

R. L. STINE

SCHOLASTIC INC.
New York Toronto London Auckland Sydney

This book is dedicated to Kristin Baker

ISBN 0-590-48744-2

Copyright © 1995 by Robert L. Stine. All rights reserved. Published by Scholastic Inc.

12 11 10 9 8 7 6 5 4　　　　　　　　5 6 7 8 9/9 0/0

Printed in the U.S.A.　　　　　01

First Scholastic printing, June 1995

The BABYSITTER IV

Prologue

"I'm back, Jenny," Mr. Hagen growled. The grin didn't waver on his fleshless, decayed face. "I'm back, and I've come for you." His black, empty eye sockets stared at her.

"No!" Jenny Jeffers cried. Her breath caught in her throat, but she forced herself to scream out her anger. "No — you're dead! You've been dead for three years!"

She stared at the tall figure. Mr. Hagen. The man who hated baby-sitters. He was crazy. Totally crazy.

Jenny had been the Hagens' baby-sitter.

Until Mr. Hagen had tried to kill her.

But she had lived. And he had died.

For three years, the memory of the horror had followed Jenny. Haunted her. Until it had driven Jenny over the edge. Until it had taken away all reality. Until the real world had vanished behind a cloud of frightening fantasy.

It had been too much. Too much for a six-teen-year-old girl to bear. And so Jenny had retreated, retreated into a world of angry dreams.

A world without time. Without warmth. Without color.

A dark world of anger. And fear.

And now he was back.

Back from the grave.

Mr. Hagen's rotting body stood grinning at her. Threatening her again. "I'm back," he announced. His voice harsh and dry, like the scrape of dead leaves.

"I've come back for you, Jenny."

"No!" she screamed, feeling her anger burn into rage. Feeling all of her muscles tighten. Her chest about to burst.

"No! You're dead! You're dead!"

She raised the silvery metal baseball bat. It felt surprisingly light in her hands.

She leaped forward. Swung hard.

The bat made a satisfying *thud* as it caught him hard in the midsection.

His body bent in reaction. The big arms flayed out. The decaying head bobbed.

With a grunt of effort, Jenny pulled the bat back. Swung again. Harder this time.

The bat made a soft *thwock* as it smashed into his face. His body whipped around. The legs buckled. The arms swayed lifelessly at his sides.

"You're *dead*!" Jenny shrieked. "Dead! Dead! Dead!"

Another hard swing sent him spinning. Jenny uttered an angry cry. Sent the bat crashing into his back. Another hard blow to the shoulder. Another blow to the back of the skull.

"You're dead! You're *dead*!" she screamed with each swing.

Mr. Hagen bobbed and twisted. Helpless against her furious attack. His head tilted back. The stuffing fell from an open tear in his chest, scattering over the grass.

Again. Again.

Jenny continued to batter him, shouting out her anger, letting out all of her fury.

"Very good, Jenny."

Dr. Morton placed a calming hand on her shoulder. He had been taking care of Jenny since she had been admitted to the hospital a year ago.

Jenny let the bat fall from her hands. She struggled to catch her breath. Her entire body trembled. Beads of hot sweat ran down her face.

"Now you are really getting into it," Dr.

Morton said, bending to pick up the bat. His white lab coat fluttered in the breeze. "You are learning how to get those angry feelings out, aren't you?"

Still breathing hard, Jenny nodded. She raised her eyes to the battered dummy, swinging from the low tree branch. The painted grin on the pillow head was all lopsided now.

"I really did knock the stuffing out of it," she declared. Shreds of white foam rubber lay scattered over the ground.

Dr. Morton tapped the end of the bat against the dummy's torn chest. "I don't think this guy will bother you again." He flashed her a smile as he pushed his glasses up on his nose. "How do you feel, Jenny?"

"Much better," she replied quickly. She turned and started to follow him back into the hospital. "I think I hit a few home runs."

I *do* feel much better, Jenny told herself. The anger, the fear — the incredible fear — it's all gone.

I'm almost ready to leave this hospital and go home, she realized happily.

And I'm never going to be afraid again.

Never.

Chapter 1

"BOO!" The hideous green face pressed up against Jenny's cheek.

Jenny groaned and rolled her eyes.

"Rick, give us a break!" Claire exclaimed. "That mask is totally gross."

"Totally," Rick repeated. He set the mask down on the display counter. Then he brushed his curly, black hair back into place. "Why do you think they sell Halloween masks in the summer?" he asked.

"Oh, I know," Rick declared, answering his own question. "For bank robbers to wear."

Jenny laughed.

Claire just stared back at him. She never got Rick's jokes. "How about some food?" she suggested. "I'm starving." She pointed to the Pizza Oven, the restaurant across the broad aisle.

Jenny followed her two friends out of the

store. The three of them had been making their way slowly through the mall, checking out different stores, laughing and joking around. Not buying anything. Just hanging out.

Hanging out.

Like normal people.

It meant so much to Jenny to be back with her two best friends. Hanging out. Kidding around.

Catching up.

She had been away from her normal life for an entire year. A whole year in the hospital. A whole year missing from her life.

Now it was summer again. A summer Jenny was determined to enjoy.

No anger. No fear. A fresh start.

Rick stopped at the restaurant window and pressed his nose against the glass, startling the kids at the table inside. Claire groaned and shoved him toward the door. "Grow up," she muttered. "You're such a baby."

"Goo goo," he replied. He sucked his thumb.

Claire didn't laugh.

"Give up," Jenny told Rick. "Claire is never going to laugh at your jokes."

"I don't call that a joke," Claire said dryly.

The two of them make such a weird couple, Jenny thought, stepping into the restaurant.

Claire is so serious, and Rick never stops goofing around.

But they've been serious about each other for nearly a year, Jenny realized.

While Jenny had been in the hospital, Claire had written to her every week. And most of her letters were about Rick and how much she cared about him.

Jenny watched Claire slide into the red vinyl booth. Claire was tall and thin, nearly a foot taller than Jenny. She had straight, brown hair, which she had streaked with blond this summer. She had it tied back into a long ponytail. She wore a pale blue tank top over white tennis shorts.

Rick piled in after her, bumping her with his shoulder, sliding until he squeezed her against the wall. "Move over! There's no room!" he cried. "Wow, are you getting fat!"

"Ha-ha," Claire replied. She elbowed him in the ribs, forcing him to edge away.

Rick pushed back his thick, black hair with one hand. He never brushed his hair, just shoved it back. He was a big teddy bear. Kind of good-looking, Jenny thought, with that broad forehead and those dark, playful eyes.

Jenny slid in across from them. She took a deep breath, inhaling the sweet aroma of cheese and tomato sauce. "The pizza in the hospital was terrible," she told them. "It was soft and doughy. And I think they used fake cheese."

"It comes from cardboard cows," Rick joked.

Jenny and Claire ignored him.

A young, blond waitress stepped up to the booth, adjusting the sleeves of her red-and-white-checked uniform. "What can I get you?"

"Do you have any fake cheese?" Rick asked.

The waitress narrowed her eyes at him. "I could check."

"Don't pay any attention to him," Claire told her. She ordered a large pepperoni pizza and a pitcher of Coke.

Jenny settled back against the seat. "Are you both working at the shoe store again this summer?" she asked. Rick's uncle owned a shoe store at the mall.

"No way!" Claire exclaimed, shaking her head. "Never again."

Rick bent down, pulled off his sneaker — a white Nike high-top — and placed it on the table. "You like it?" he asked Jenny. "I can get you a twenty percent discount."

"No thanks." Jenny laughed. "Guess you're back at the store, huh?"

Rick nodded. "Uncle Bill made me an offer I couldn't refuse. He named me assistant manager."

Claire rolled her eyes. "Rick's uncle has three salespeople. He made them all assistant managers."

"So what?" Rick cried. "I still get the assistant manager's discount."

The waitress returned with a pitcher of Coke and three glasses. She stared down at Rick's sneaker on the table.

"I'm going to drink from that," Rick told her.

The waitress didn't crack a smile. "We get a lot of funny people in here," she muttered. She set down the pitcher, turned, and strode away.

Rick blushed. Jenny and Claire laughed. Rick removed the sneaker from the table and bent to put it back on.

"The worst part about selling shoes is the lacing," Claire told Jenny, pouring the Coke into glasses. "You spend all day lacing sneakers, lacing sneakers, lacing sneakers. It takes forever. And then the customer is never happy. You laced it too loose. Too tight. Too high. Too low. Aaagggh!" She let out a cry, wrapped her hands around Rick's neck, and playfully pretended to strangle him.

"Hey — !" He pulled away from her. "Don't blame *me* if you don't have what it takes to be an assistant manager!"

Even Claire had to laugh at that.

"So where are you working this summer?" Jenny asked her.

Claire took a long sip of soda. "At the community pool."

"She's a drowning instructor!" Rick joked.

"I'm working at the food stand," Claire continued, ignoring him. "It's okay. I get to swim during my breaks. And I get to see a lot of kids from school."

Rick waved across the restaurant to some friends. "Back in a minute," he said. He slid out and made his way to their table. Jenny watched him slapping high fives and cracking jokes.

Claire's serious, brown eyes locked on Jenny. "And what are you doing this summer? Just hanging out?"

Jenny nodded. "Yeah. You know. Getting back to normal."

"How's your mom?" Claire asked.

"Really good," Jenny told her. "She got a new job, which she really likes."

"As a legal secretary?"

Jenny nodded. "Yeah. And she's been busy fixing up our new house."

"How do you like it?" Claire asked.

Jenny shrugged. "It's okay. Just kind of weird for me. You know. Getting out of the hospital and going home to a whole new neighborhood."

Jenny twirled the fork between her fingers. "Mom's really happy to have me home. Of course. And . . . guess what? She's seeing a guy."

Claire's mouth dropped open. "Your mom? That's great!" she exclaimed.

Since her divorce, Jenny's mother had been pretty lonely. Lonely and depressed.

When Jenny came home from the hospital, she knew immediately that something had changed. Her mother had darkened the gray in her hair. Her clothes were younger-looking. And she seemed so cheerful and energetic.

"Who is he?" Claire demanded. "Have you met him? Is he nice?"

Jenny snickered. "His name is Winston. Isn't that the pits?"

Claire narrowed her eyes at Jenny. "Is that his first name or his last?"

"His first," Jenny replied. "Everyone calls

him Win. I met him the other night. He seems really nice. He's very good-looking. Tanned. Blue eyes. Sort of a blond prince type. I think he's younger than she is."

"Wow," Claire murmured. "Lots of changes in your life, huh?"

Jenny sighed. "Yeah. Well . . . I've been away for a whole year, you know."

"I know," Claire replied, lowering her eyes. And then she added in a low voice, "You seem changed, too."

The comment caught Jenny by surprise. "Huh? What do you mean?"

Claire spun the Coke glass between her hands. "Better. You seem a lot better," she replied thoughtfully. "You seem stronger somehow, Jenny. More like your old self. Before . . . before . . ." Her voice trailed off.

"Before Mr. Hagen and all the horror?" Jenny finished the sentence for her friend. "Go ahead. You can say it, Claire. I'm not afraid anymore. You're right about me being changed. The year in the hospital changed me completely."

Jenny leaned across the table. She squeezed Claire's hands. "I'm not afraid anymore, Claire. I'm not afraid of anything now. I *am* much stronger. I *am* the old me."

Jenny was startled to see tears form in

Claire's eyes. "I'm glad," Claire said, wiping them away with her fingers. "I really am."

The pizza tasted delicious. The sound of normal, happy voices ringing through the crowded restaurant made Jenny feel even better.

She felt so wonderful being back with her friends, back in her real life.

Things are going to be great from now on, she promised herself. From now on . . .

But, then, as Rick dropped her off in front of her new house, as she waved good night to him and Claire, as she watched his little red Civic back down the driveway and disappear into the night, as she turned to the walk that led to her front door — Jenny saw a dark figure step out from the shadows at the side of the house.

Chapter 2

She gasped. Felt a chill of fear.

No!

No! she told herself. I'm not afraid.

No more running from shadows.

She took a deep breath, then walked toward the figure. He stepped into the pale light from the porch.

"Cal!" Jenny cried. "What are you doing here?"

He hurried across the driveway to her. She threw her arms around him, hugged him close.

They kissed.

A whole year without any kisses, she thought, keeping her eyes open, wanting to see him, wanting to stare into those pale blue eyes of his.

A whole year without kisses. Is that why Cal and I have gotten so much closer? Is that why our relationship has become so intense?

She and Cal had been seeing each other before the horrible events of last summer. But she hadn't felt so deeply about him then.

She hugged him tighter. Took a deep breath. Kissed him again.

I'm so grateful for Cal, Jenny thought. He stayed with me. He didn't abandon me. He wrote to me. The letters we wrote to each other helped me so much, helped me to remember that I had a real life waiting for me back home.

Cal gave me a good reason to get out of the hospital. And stay out.

I'm going to stay healthy for you, Cal, Jenny promised silently, stroking the back of his white-blond hair. I'm going to stay brave for you, Cal.

When they finished the kiss, they both were breathless.

"Sorry," Cal whispered. "Sorry I didn't meet you guys at the mall."

"Where were you?" Jenny asked softly, holding his hand between hers.

"Had to work an extra shift," Cal told her with a sigh. The tiny gold stud in his ear caught the light from the porch. "One of the guys was sick. So you-know-who gets to stay and pump gas."

She let go of his hand and leaned against

him. His T-shirt smelled of gasoline. So did his hands. "At least you have a job this summer," she murmured.

"Yeah. I guess."

She pressed both hands against the front of his shirt. His chest felt so solid. "You won't have to work Saturday night — right?"

He nodded. "I already told Hansen. He gave me a hard time. Do you believe it? Like I haven't worked double shifts for the guy all week."

Cal shook his head. Jenny saw a flash of anger in his eyes. "Man, I hate that guy!" Cal exploded. "He thinks he's hot stuff because he owns one lousy gas station."

Jenny raised a hand to his shoulder to calm him. But Cal shook it away.

"He doesn't even *own* the station," he continued bitterly. "His brother-in-law owns it. But Hansen thinks he's king of the world. You should hear him yelling at me because I left the cash register open."

"Cal — please!" Jenny insisted quietly. She hated when Cal went into one of his rages. Normally, he was so quiet. But he had an angry side. Jenny never knew what might touch it off, make him explode with rage.

Cal always managed to get himself in control. But it frightened Jenny. It frightened her a lot. And it made her think there was a whole side of Cal — an angry, bitter side — she didn't know at all.

"We're going out Saturday night, and that's that!" Cal said heatedly. "And if Hansen tells me I have to work late, I — I'll just quit."

"No, you won't," Jenny replied quickly. "You won't quit," she scolded. "You need the money, and you know it."

Cal's dad had been laid off from the box factory where he was a foreman. The family was living on his mom's salary as assistant store manager at Wal-Mart.

"Stop talking so crazy and kiss me good night," Jenny instructed.

The kiss lasted a long time.

When it ended, Jenny pushed herself away from him with both hands. "See you," she murmured breathlessly. And ran into her house without glancing back.

Jenny's mother had gone to bed. The house was dark except for the front entry light.

Jenny made her way quickly up the stairs to her room. She clicked on the ceiling light and stepped inside.

The sheer white curtains over her bedroom window fluttered in a light breeze. She let her eyes wander slowly around the room. It was still unfamiliar to her. Everything was so clean. So bright. So . . . *nice*.

The hospital cot had been narrow and hard. The nurses tucked the scratchy sheets in so tightly, Jenny had trouble getting under them.

Jenny dropped onto her soft bedspread, remembering.

In the hospital, she had shared a room with five other girls. No privacy. Some of them, she remembered, cried at night. Every night.

The phone rang, jolting Jenny from her unhappy memories.

She glanced at the bed table clock. Nearly midnight.

Who would be calling this late?

Mr. Hagen!

She couldn't help it. She couldn't keep the frightening memories from flooding back.

Mr. Hagen. He had always called so late. In his cruel, raspy whisper. *"Company's coming, Babes."* The cold, terrifying threat.

"Company's coming."

The phone rang again. So loud in the deep silence of the house.

Jenny reached for the receiver.

She hesitated.

Should she pick it up?

Chapter 3

It's not going to be Mr. Hagen! she told herself.

I'm not going to be afraid to pick up the phone ever again.

She grabbed the receiver before it could ring a third time and raised it to her ear. "Hello?"

"Hi, Jen."

"Claire?"

"Yeah. It's me."

"What's wrong, Claire?" Jenny asked. "Why are you — "

"Just wondered if you were okay," Claire replied. She yawned loudly.

"Well, of course," Jenny told her. "I'm fine. I don't understand — "

"I called a few minutes ago, and you didn't answer," Claire said sleepily. "So I got kind of worried. I mean, Rick and I dropped you off at least half an hour ago. So I figured — "

Jenny laughed. "I was out front. With Cal."

19

Silence at Claire's end. Then: "Oh. I see."

"He had to work late. That's why he didn't meet us," Jenny explained. "He was waiting when I got home, and . . ." Her voice trailed off.

"Okay. Sorry. I was just a little worried," Claire replied. "How come your mom didn't answer the phone?"

"You know what a heavy sleeper she is," Jenny told her. "She once slept through a tornado. Really!"

"Well . . . okay," Claire said. "I — I just wanted to say it was great. I mean, tonight, Jen. I mean, it's just so great having you back. Really."

"Thanks, Claire," Jenny choked out. She felt a wave of emotion sweep over her. "You're a good friend. But I don't want you to worry about me. I'm going to be fine. From now on."

"I know," Claire replied softly. "But, listen, Jen. If there's anything . . . anything stressing you out, or anything messing up your mind. Anything you want to talk about . . . well . . . you know you can talk to me — right?"

"Thanks, Claire," Jenny repeated. "You've been great."

She said good night and hung up the phone.

A few minutes later, she clicked off the light and settled into her soft, clean, comfortable bed. Her head sank into the soft down pillow.

Before I was in the hospital, she realized, I never noticed things like a pillow or a soft bed. I took everything for granted. Everything. But, now, everything makes me happy. All the little things I never noticed — they all make me happy.

Jenny was about to drift into sleep when she heard the first howl.

It's the wind through the trees, she told herself drowsily.

The second howl made her sit up.

An animal howl. Filled with anger. And pain.

She lowered her feet to the floor. Turned toward the window, to the fluttering curtains. Listened intently.

Another long, low animal howl.

Jenny shivered. "What's making that cry?" she wondered out loud.

She stood up and tiptoed to the window.

Chapter 4

Pushing the curtains aside, Jenny poked her head out of the window and peered down.

White moonlight washed over the backyard, making the lawn gleam like silver. A large green watering can lay on its side near her mother's flower garden. The garden hose sat coiled like a snake beside the garage wall.

Another low howl.

So cold. So hollow-sounding.

Jenny lowered her eyes toward it.

And caught a glimpse of someone. Or something. Flitting across the grass.

A boy?

Blond hair?

A little boy?

Huh?

A wind gust blew the curtain over her face. The soft fabric tickled her skin. She pulled the curtain away with both hands.

Peered down.

No one there now.

No blond-haired boy.

No one. Nothing moving. And not a sound. Except for faint music. Someone playing music several houses away.

No howls. No boy scampering across the back lawn.

Jenny, you always had a good imagination, she told herself.

Letting the curtains slide over her, she turned and strode back to bed.

She met the Warsaw kids the next afternoon.

A sultry summer day. The grass felt hot and dry beneath her bare feet. Jenny wore a faded pink midriff top and denim cutoffs cut very short. She had tied her brown hair up in a bun to keep it off her back.

Carrying a can of iced tea and a paperback mystery novel, she made her way to the broad sassafras tree in the middle of the backyard. She settled in the shade, leaning her back against the smooth tree trunk, and set the iced-tea can beside her on the grass.

Two black-and-yellow monarch butterflies fluttered over the geraniums in her mother's garden. It was a lot cooler beneath the tree,

Jenny realized happily. And the grass smelled fragrant and sweet.

Jenny heard a metallic jangle. The jangle of dog tags. A big German shepherd poked its head out from the side of the garage.

"How are you, boy?" Jenny called.

She had seen the dog before. He lived across the street. He lumbered over, his bushy tail wagging. He let Jenny stroke his back for a few seconds. Then he wandered off toward the front of the house.

She gazed around the backyard contentedly. The watering can on its side and the coiled garden hose brought back the memory of the night before. The strange howls. The little blond boy.

But the memory had lost its fear for Jenny.

I was half-asleep, she told herself. I probably heard someone's TV. I didn't see a boy in the yard. I saw shadows, tossed by the wind.

The first thing Jenny had learned in the hospital was not to frighten herself.

As soon as she had learned that, as soon as she had learned to lock her mind on cold reality, to keep her mind from creating its own horrors — she started to recover.

Even the nightmares had stopped.

What haunting, chilling nightmares she had

suffered through! Stomach-churning scenes of Mr. Hagen pulling himself up from the grave. Mr. Hagen. Staggering toward Jenny, his skeletal hands outstretched, the decaying skin falling off in clumps from his eyeless skull.

Hideous, hideous dreams — dreams so real, they had made Jenny wake up shrieking, drenched in cold sweat, morning after morning.

But no more.

Not a single nightmare.

Because she lived in the real world now.

Jenny took a long sip of the iced tea. She rubbed the cold can against her temples. Then she set it down beside her and opened her book.

A high-pitched giggle from the next yard made her turn her eyes to the fence. A white picket fence separated the Jefferses' new house from the neighbors'.

The fence needed a paint job, Jenny saw. The paint was faded and peeling. A few of the boards were cracked and tilting at odd angles.

Jenny heard another laugh. Then excited cries.

Kids. A boy and a girl? Two boys?

Jenny's mom had reported that new neighbors had moved into the house next door. But Jenny hadn't met them yet.

She felt tempted to get up and go peer over the fence. But she was too comfortable. She raised the book and started to read.

She had read only a paragraph when she heard her name being called. "Jenny? Are you Jenny?"

Gazing up, Jenny saw a woman leaning on the fence from the next yard. She had her arms resting on the fence. Her face was round, circled by tight ringlets of light brown hair.

"Are you Jenny?" the woman repeated. She had a tiny, little girl's voice. Sort of a cartoon voice, Jenny thought. Jenny couldn't guess her age. Somewhere between thirty and forty.

"Uh . . . hi." Jenny climbed slowly to her feet, being careful not to spill the iced tea.

"I'm Mrs. Warsaw," the woman said. "I met your mother, but I haven't met you."

Jenny heard angry shouts from behind the fence. The kids were fighting about something. Mrs. Warsaw turned away to break it up.

When the angry shouting ended, the woman turned back to Jenny. "Nice to meet you," Jenny said awkwardly. "It's such a hot day, I — " She motioned to the tree.

"Can you do me a favor?" Mrs. Warsaw asked. She brushed a fly off her face with a chubby hand. The sun made the tight ringlets around her face gleam.

"A favor?" Jenny asked. She took a few steps closer to the fence. The grass felt hot beneath her bare feet.

"I have to run to the store," Mrs. Warsaw said, turning to glance back at the kids. "Could you come over here and watch them for a few minutes?"

More shouts.

The woman turned to the kids again. "Sean. Meredith. What are you doing now?"

Jenny swallowed hard.

She's asking me to baby-sit, she realized. She struggled to fight the dread away, to fight back the memories that threatened to invade her mind.

"I'll be back in five minutes," Mrs. Warsaw promised in her tiny mouse voice. "Ten or fifteen at the most. I'm really sorry to trouble you. But there's no one else I can ask."

"Well . . ." Jenny hesitated.

Mrs. Warsaw sighed. "I can't really afford a full-time baby-sitter. You understand. I'm usually home during the day. So it's no problem. But, today . . ."

Jenny took a deep breath. "I'll come right over," she said.

"Oh, thanks! Thanks so much! You're a doll!" Mrs. Warsaw cried gratefully. "They're good kids. They'll just play outside till I get back. Thanks, Jenny. I really appreciate it."

"No problem," Jenny murmured.

She picked up her iced-tea can and started to make her way around the fence.

I'm baby-sitting, she thought.

My troubles always started when I was baby-sitting.

But it's only for ten minutes.

I'll be fine. I'll be perfectly fine.

Won't I?

Chapter 5

Jenny stepped into the Warsaws' yard. Mrs. Warsaw had already climbed into her car, a green Taurus.

"Sean! Meredith! Don't fight!" she called. "Be nice to Jenny, okay?" She slammed the car door shut and backed down the gravel driveway.

Jenny turned to the kids. Sean was eight or nine. He was skinny and pale, almost frail-looking. He stared at Jenny through large brown eyes. Solemn eyes.

Sean's white-blond hair fell carelessly down to his collar. He wore an oversized T-shirt and baggy denim shorts, which made him look even skinnier.

Meredith squeezed a yellow tennis ball between her chubby hands. She was five or six, plump, with a round face like her mother's. She had curly, light brown hair tied back in a loose ponytail, and tiny dark eyes close together around a pudgy stub of a nose.

Meredith wore a sleeveless yellow T-shirt and matching yellow shorts. Her sneakers were yellow, too.

She's not very pretty, Jenny thought, staring back at her.

Meredith had a red scratch across one chubby knee. She had a small Band-Aid on her chin. Beads of sweat glistened above her upper lip.

"Hi, guys," Jenny greeted them cheerfully. "What's up?"

Sean pointed. "You're barefoot."

Jenny nodded, glancing down at her feet. "Yeah. I know."

"Mom says it's dangerous to go barefoot," Sean declared. "You could step on something and cut your foot."

"I cut *my* foot last summer," Meredith announced, squeezing the tennis ball in her hand. She slapped at a horsefly on the back of her left leg. "Ow!"

"I'll be careful," Jenny told them. "It's such a hot day, I thought — "

The screen door slammed. Jenny turned to the back of the house in time to see another boy step out of the kitchen.

"Here comes Seth," Sean said.

"Hey — he's your twin!" Jenny exclaimed.
Sean nodded.

Jenny saw at once that Sean and Seth were identical twins. Seth had the same white-blond hair, the same solemn, brown eyes. He had the same slender, frail build, the same pale skin.

He came running up to Jenny and smiled at her. "Hi, I'm Seth." His voice was softer than Sean's, younger somehow.

"I'm Jenny," she greeted him. She glanced quickly from one boy to the other. "How can I tell you guys apart?"

"You can't," Sean replied casually.

Seth laughed. Sean's expression remained stern.

Sean isn't terribly friendly, Jenny thought. Maybe he's shy.

"Do you live next door?" Seth asked, pointing to the fence.

Jenny nodded. "Yeah." She turned to the Warsaws' house. It was a white clapboard box, two stories high, with a small attic. A gray slate roof with an old TV antenna still clinging to the chimney.

"Do you like your new house?" Jenny asked the kids.

"No," Meredith and Sean replied in unison.

Jenny laughed. "Why not?"

"Because it's haunted," Sean told her.

Was he making a joke? Jenny waited for him to smile. But Sean's expression remained as serious as ever.

"Sean believes in ghosts," Seth said, grinning. "He's kind of spooky."

"It *is* haunted!" Meredith insisted. "The house is haunted, and you know it, Seth!"

"Shut up, Piggy!" Sean shouted at his sister.

"*You* shut up!" Meredith shot back in a shrill whine. "And don't call me Piggy!"

Seth smiled up at Jenny. "They always fight like that," he explained to her. "No big deal."

Meredith glared angrily at Sean. Then she turned to Jenny, a devilish grin spreading over her round face. "When Sean was little, Mommy used to call him Bunny Rabbit."

"Shut up!" Sean screamed. "I mean it, Meredith! Shut up!"

Meredith's grin grew wider. She ignored her brother and kept her gaze on Jenny. "Mommy called him Bunny Rabbit because he was so tiny and pale, he looked like a little bunny rabbit."

Meredith let out a mean laugh.

Sean's face turned bright pink. "I said *shut up!*" he screamed.

He dove at Meredith angrily.

Still laughing, she ducked away and started to run.

With an angry cry, Sean ran after her. He caught her easily. Tackled her from behind. Landed on top of her. And began furiously pounding her back with both fists.

Thrashing her arms helplessly, Meredith started to scream and cry.

"Hey — stop!" Jenny shouted, running over to them.

Seth got there first. He struggled to pull his brother away. "Whoa. Come on. Whoa!" he urged.

Jenny slid her hands under Sean's armpits and lifted him off his sister. "Stop it, Sean!" she insisted. "Calm down — okay?" He feels so light, Jenny thought. Like picking up a feather pillow.

Meredith climbed to her feet and rubbed at the grass stains on her knees. "Sean, you're so dumb," she muttered.

Jenny set Sean back down on his feet. "You shouldn't hit your sister like that," she scolded.

"I didn't hurt her!" Sean protested angrily. He walked across the grass and picked up the tennis ball.

"Hey — that's mine!" Meredith called.

Seth stepped up close to Jenny. "They do this all the time," he said softly. "But it's no big deal. Really."

"Aren't they ever nice to each other?" Jenny whispered.

"Sometimes," Seth replied, flashing her a sweet smile. He trotted across the grass to play catch with Sean.

The twins are certainly different, Jenny thought. She felt drawn to Seth immediately. He seemed so sweet and calm. And kind.

Jenny studied Sean. Lots of brothers don't get along with their little sisters, she knew. But Sean seemed so angry, so ready to explode at any moment. He started screaming for Meredith to shut up before she had hardly said a word.

Why was Meredith so eager to tell that Bunny Rabbit story about Sean? Jenny wondered. Why was she so eager to embarrass Sean and make him angry?

Jenny sighed.

Kids, she thought.

Kids are definitely weird.

The twins were playing catch, tossing the tennis ball as high as they could, sending high fly balls to each other across the yard.

"Give me my ball back!" Meredith demanded. She ran into Sean — charging like a bull — and made him miss the ball. Then the two of them scrambled over the grass to grab it.

"Hey, I've got an idea!" Jenny called. She reached out her hands. "Toss me the ball. We'll play a game. All of us. Okay?"

"Cool!" Seth cried with enthusiasm.

"What kind of game?" Sean asked skeptically.

Jenny taught them how to play Slap Ball. She was the pitcher. She bounced the tennis ball — one bounce — to the batter, who slapped the ball with an open hand. Since they didn't have enough players for teams, they just took batting practice.

The three kids liked the game. They all got along really well.

Jenny felt almost sorry when Mrs. Warsaw returned a few minutes later. She was just starting to warm up to the kids and feel comfortable with them.

Seth and Meredith seem to like me, Jenny realized. Sean was a tough cookie. He would still take some work.

As Mrs. Warsaw opened her car door, Seth disappeared into the house. Sean and Meredith went running to the car to greet their mother.

"How'd it go?" Mrs. Warsaw called to Jenny.

"Fine. Just fine," Jenny replied. She hurried to help Mrs. Warsaw carry her groceries into the house.

"Jenny's nice," Meredith told her mother.

Mrs. Warsaw turned to Sean. "Do you like Jenny, too?"

Sean shrugged his slender shoulders. "She's okay."

Mrs. Warsaw winked at Jenny. "High praise," she commented.

Jenny laughed. She carried a grocery bag into the kitchen and set it down on the counter. Then she glanced around the room. The kitchen was cluttered and cramped. The flowery wallpaper had faded, and one corner curled down from the ceiling over the stove.

A small, black table radio on the counter had been left on, tuned low to a country station. Dirty dish towels had been tossed in a pile beside it.

When the groceries had all been brought in, Jenny turned to go.

"Wait. Let me pay you," Mrs. Warsaw insisted, grabbing Jenny's arm.

"Huh? Pay me?" The thought caught Jenny by surprise. "No way, Mrs. Warsaw. It was just fifteen minutes. You really don't have to — "

"But I want to," the woman replied, picking

up one of the soiled dish towels and folding it.

"No. Really." Jenny backed to the kitchen door. "I won't take any money."

Mrs. Warsaw picked up another towel and started to fold it. "Well, next time," she said. She set down the towel. "At least let me get you a cold drink. A soda or something."

"Uh . . . okay. That would be great!" Jenny replied. "It's so hot out there. We were playing ball, and — "

"The kids really seem to like you," Mrs. Warsaw said, pulling open the refrigerator door and bending to reach the soda cans.

A loud scream from the front of the house made her pull herself up straight. "Mommy — he's *hitting* me again!" Meredith's shrill wail rose through the house like a police siren.

"Be right back." Shaking her head, Mrs. Warsaw hurried out of the kitchen to go stop the battle.

Jenny leaned one hand on the counter. The voice on the radio was announcing the weather forecast. More of the same. Hot and humid. Behind her, she could hear Mrs. Warsaw scolding the kids somewhere at the other end of the house.

A cloud rolled over the sun. The room darkened.

Jenny turned to the kitchen window. Staring

out, she could see her house rising up on the other side of the fence. I wonder if Mom is home from work, Jenny thought.

She was still staring out the window when she felt the icy hand on the back of her neck. Felt the cold, cold fingers slide wetly down her back.

Chapter 6

With a startled cry, Jenny spun around.

"Huh?"

No one there.

She shivered. She could still feel the cold on her back.

She could still feel the wet fingers sliding around her neck.

"Hey — who did that?" she cried in a shaky voice. She rubbed the back of her neck, trying to smooth the lingering cold away. Then she ducked down and peered around the side of the counter.

Expecting to see Sean. Or Seth. Or even Meredith.

But no. No one there.

She could hear the kids arguing with their mother in the other room. It couldn't have been them.

So who touched me? Jenny asked herself.

Who slid that cold hand down my back?

She stood up. Her eyes searched the small kitchen one more time. Such a cold feeling still there, she realized. A cold presence.

Feeling shaken, she made her way to the screen door. "Mrs. Warsaw — " she called loudly. "I have to go home now! Bye!"

Jenny pushed the door open and ran out into the yard. The door slammed behind her. The yard was bathed in shade. Clouds rolled rapidly overhead. As if speeded up. As if set into fast forward.

Jenny blinked, waiting for her eyes to adjust. She turned back to the house.

And saw a face staring out at her.

A face up at the top of the house. In the narrow attic window.

"Wh-who's that?" she stammered out loud.

A boy? A girl?

She could see dark eyes. See a forehead topped by dark hair.

Not one of the kids, she thought.

Not anyone I've seen before.

Who could be up in the attic? Who could be up there staring down at me like that?

Bright sunlight rolled over the lawn, sweeping away the shade. Sunlight filled the attic window. Made it gleam like gold.

Jenny shielded her eyes.

When the light faded, she raised her eyes once more to the window.

The face had vanished.

Only darkness up there now.

A trick of the light? Jenny wondered, standing in the middle of the yard, squinting up at the narrow window.

Just light and shadows — like the man in the moon?

Or was it a real face I saw? Someone staring down at me, watching me so intently.

Chapter 7

"I'm fine," Jenny said.

"Glad to hear it." Dr. Simonson flashed her a smile and motioned to the leather couch. "You look really well, Jenny. Have you been getting some sun?"

"Just in the backyard," Jenny replied. She settled on to the couch. Her eyes went to the framed diplomas on the wall behind Dr. Simonson's desk.

The psychiatrist pushed a strand of gray hair off her forehead as she lowered herself into her desk chair. She was a small, pleasant woman, in her early sixties. Jenny had come to love her soft, soothing voice, her large blue sympathetic eyes. Her thoughtfulness. Her calm.

Someday I'd like to be calm like her, Jenny often thought. I'd like to pause and take a moment to think before saying anything. I'd like to be wise like Dr. Simonson. And kind.

"How is your mother doing?" Dr. Simonson asked, turning pages on her writing pad.

"Okay," Jenny replied. "She's very glad to have me back."

"I should think so!" the doctor exclaimed. She leaned forward, her eyes studying Jenny. "So? Anything to tell me? Problems? Dreams?"

Jenny shook her head. "No bad dreams. Not one."

Dr. Simonson smiled and nodded her head. She glanced at her desk clock. "Tell me about your week. Try to make it interesting. I just had a session with my most boring patient. She insists on telling me about her ingrown toenails!"

Jenny laughed. "Maybe she thinks you're a foot doctor."

"Maybe I *am* a foot doctor!" Dr. Simonson joked. "Heads. Feet. What's the difference?"

Jenny took a deep breath and tried to recall all that had happened to her in the past week. She talked about Claire. And Rick. And Cal. About getting used to her new house. And about baby-sitting for the new kids next door.

That aroused Dr. Simonson's interest. She set down her pen and studied Jenny. "How did that go?"

"Fine," Jenny told her with a shrug. "The kids don't get along that well. But they're okay."

"You felt comfortable?" the doctor asked.

Jenny thought about it. "Yes. Fine."

Dr. Simonson gave her an approving nod. "Sounds good, Jenny. It all sounds good." She cleared her throat. Checked the clock again. "So what scared you this week?"

"Excuse me?" The question caught Jenny by surprise.

"What scared you, Jenny? There must have been something."

"When I was alone in the Warsaws' kitchen, I felt a presence. A cold presence. I felt cold fingers on the back of my neck. When I turned around, there was no one there. And when I went outside, I saw someone up in the attic, someone I had never seen before, staring down at me."

Those were the words Jenny *wanted* to say.

Those were the words that were about to burst out.

But she held them back. She forced herself not to say them.

She didn't want to tell Dr. Simonson about the icy hand, the strange face in the attic.

She didn't want to tell Dr. Simonson anything to make her think that Jenny wasn't one hundred percent okay.

Because I *am* okay, Jenny told herself. And no one is going to tell me that I'm not.

"I'm fine," she told Dr. Simonson, returning the doctor's unblinking stare. "Perfectly fine. Nothing scared me this week. Nothing at all."

After her doctor appointment, Jenny drove to the community pool and visited Claire. It was a cloudy day, threatening rain. Jenny found the pool nearly empty. There were few customers for the food stand, so Claire had plenty of time to talk.

It started to drizzle a little before five. A warm, summer rain that made the air heavy and steamy.

Jenny drove to the mall and picked up a few items her mother had asked for. She thought about dropping into the shoe store to visit Rick. But it was nearly dinnertime. She didn't want to keep her mother waiting.

At a little after six, she pulled the car into the garage. She made her way into the kitchen to find Mrs. Warsaw seated at the counter, finishing a cup of tea.

Jenny's mom hurried over to take the packages from Jenny's arms. "Did you get soaked?" she asked.

Jenny cheerfully shook her head. "The rain felt good, actually."

"Good timing," Mrs. Warsaw declared, shoving the cup and saucer away. "I was just asking your mom if you can stay with the kids tonight."

Jenny turned to her mom. "Baby-sit?"

Mrs. Jeffers bit her lower lip. Her dark eyes locked on Jenny. "Only if you feel like it."

"I won't be out late," Mrs. Warsaw added. "I know this is so last minute. But I couldn't find anyone else."

"I'll be right next door," Mrs. Jeffers told Jenny. "If anything happens, I'm five seconds away."

Jenny hesitated.

Her mother stared at her with concern. "But if it will make you uncomfortable, dear . . . feel free to say no. I'm sure Mrs. Warsaw will understand."

"The kids really liked you," Mrs. Warsaw said. She pulled a thread off her pink and blue sundress. "They begged me to get you to stay with them."

"It's up to you, Jen. Really," her mother insisted.

Jenny turned to Mrs. Warsaw. "What time do you need me?"

A smile burst across Mrs. Warsaw's round face. "Seven o'clock?"

"See you then," Jenny replied.

You'll be okay, she told herself.

You'll be okay from now on.

It's just a baby-sitting job, Jenny thought. What could happen?

Chapter 8

"They won't let me play!" Meredith whined. "Make them give me a turn!"

The twins had hooked the Super-Nintendo to the TV in the living room and were intensely involved in a video hockey game.

"Can't you turn it down a little?" Jenny pleaded.

The volume was turned way up. The synthetic game music repeated endlessly, competing with the *slap slap slap* of the puck.

"Did you boys hear me?"

They continued feverishly maneuvering their controllers, ignoring her.

Jenny climbed up from the armchair and strode to the TV set, blocking their view.

"Hey — !"

"Move away!"

"Are you going to give Meredith a turn?" Jenny demanded, refusing to budge.

"Meredith doesn't like hockey," Sean replied. Jenny knew it was Sean from his voice, harsher, deeper than Seth's. And because Sean was always the one being nasty to Meredith.

Otherwise, there really was no way to tell them apart. Tonight the boys were even dressed alike, in oversized dark blue T-shirts and faded denim cutoffs.

"Let me play one of *my* games!" Meredith insisted.

"Your games are too babyish," Sean replied. He frantically waved both hands, trying to persuade Jenny to move out of the way.

"You can have a turn when the hockey game is over," Seth suggested.

"Well, hurry up!" Meredith demanded.

Jenny stepped away from the front of the TV. "That was nice of you, Seth," she said, patting his blond head as she made her way past the boys to the armchair.

"Seth is a *nice* boy!" Sean declared sarcastically. He reached over and tickled his twin in the ribs. "Nice boy! Such a nice boy!"

Seth jerked out of Sean's reach. He continued moving his controller. A cheer went up on the screen. The music played a fanfare.

"Goal!" Seth screamed. "Goal!" He stuck his tongue out at Sean.

"It doesn't count!" Sean declared angrily. "I was tickling you. I wasn't watching!"

"It counts!" Seth argued. "You lose. You lose big."

Jenny dropped back into the armchair. She turned to Meredith. "I forgot to ask your mom about bedtimes. When do you guys go to bed?"

"Seth and I go at midnight!" Sean replied, grinning at Seth. "Meredith's bedtime is *now!*"

"It is not!" Meredith protested. "You're a jerk, Sean."

"You're a bigger jerk!" Sean shot back.

Jenny raised both hands in a "halt" sign. "Come on, guys," she pleaded. "I asked a simple question. When is bedtime?"

"I go at eight-thirty," Meredith told her. "Sean and Seth — they go at nine." And then she added, "But they never do."

Jenny laughed. For some reason, Meredith's serious expression struck her funny. Before long, they were all laughing. Jenny wasn't sure why. But they all started laughing at once, and couldn't stop.

She had fun with them for the rest of the evening.

They played several long games of *Uno*. Meredith had trouble keeping the rules of the card game straight, but Jenny helped her. And for once, Sean wasn't mean to her.

Jenny gave them all ice-cream bars for a late snack.

They watched a little TV, channel-surfing from station to station, not finding anything the kids were interested in.

And then Jenny managed to get them upstairs to their bedrooms by nine-thirty.

Meredith had a tiny pink room, no bigger than a clothes closet. Her bed stretched across the back of the room under the window. One entire wall contained built-in shelves up to the ceiling. They were jammed with books, and games, and dozens of dolls and stuffed animals.

Jenny tucked her in and clicked off the overhead light. Then she made her way down the hall to the twins' room. Their room wasn't much larger, just big enough to hold bunk beds, a small desk, and a dresser.

Jenny reached to turn out the light.

"I'm not tired," Sean insisted. "I want to stay up later."

"Get into bed," Jenny replied sternly. "It's late, Sean."

"But I'm not tired!" he protested.

"I'm tired," Seth said, yawning. He was already tucked into the upper bunk. "Come on, Sean. Give Jenny a break."

Sean reluctantly obeyed his brother.

Seth is such a good kid, Jenny thought gratefully. He's been so sweet.

She clicked out the light and turned to leave their bedroom — when she heard the sound.

A creaking. Overhead.

Swallowing hard, Jenny stopped in the doorway, half in the bedroom, half in the dimly lit hall.

And listened.

She heard it again. Floorboards creaking.

First one direction. Then back.

Footsteps.

Feeling a chill of fright, she raised her eyes to the ceiling.

And heard the sound again.

Someone is up there, Jenny realized, gripped with fear.

Someone is up in the attic.

Chapter 9

Jenny turned back to the boys. "Did you hear anything?" she asked in a trembling voice.

They both sat up. "Hear what?" Sean demanded.

"Uh . . ." Jenny hesitated. She didn't want to frighten them.

But then the ceiling groaned. The footsteps were right overhead.

"Did you hear that?" Jenny blurted out. "Up in the attic?"

"It's nothing," Seth assured her. "We always hear noises at night — don't we, Sean?"

"Yeah," his brother agreed, yawning.

"Are you scared, Jenny?" Seth asked softly.

"No," Jenny answered quickly.

What am I doing? she scolded herself. I don't want to scare the boys because the ceiling is creaking.

"Uh . . . good night, guys," she said, turning into the hall. "Sweet dreams."

She took a few steps along the narrow hallway. Then she stopped and listened again.

Creak . . . creeeeeak . . .

There's someone walking back and forth up there, Jenny decided.

She took a deep breath and held it. I'm not going to let my fear run away with me, she told herself. She remembered the important lessons she had learned in the hospital.

She fought back the panic that froze her.

I'm in charge here, she told herself. I'm in control.

She gazed around the narrow hallway. A single dim floor lamp at the other end of the hall provided the only light. The shadow of a narrow table stretched across the carpet like two bony arms.

Creeeeeak . . . creak . . .

Maybe an animal climbed into the attic, she decided.

A squirrel. Or a raccoon.

She remembered the time a squirrel had somehow found its way into the attic in her old house. Jenny was a little girl. Her father was still living with them. He chased after the squirrel with a fishing net.

Every time Mr. Jeffers swung the net, the

squirrel darted away. Back and forth, her father chased the squirrel through the cluttered attic. Furniture crashed to the floor. A pile of cartons toppled over.

Her father went into a rage, screaming at the squirrel, swinging the net wildly. And the angrier he got, the harder Jenny laughed.

He just looked so funny. A big bear of a man chasing after a tiny, scrawny, frightened squirrel.

Finally, Jenny remembered, when the attic was totally destroyed and her father was red-faced and gasping for air, the squirrel casually hopped out the window and disappeared.

Recalling that long-ago day brought a smile to Jenny's face.

Creeeeak. Creeeak.

The sounds above her head snapped her from her memories. It's just a squirrel, she decided. I'm not afraid. I'll go check it out.

She crossed the hall to the doorway that led up to the attic.

She reached for the glass doorknob.

And felt a bony hand slide against her waist.

Chapter 10

"Ohhh!"

Jenny uttered a startled cry.

She turned to see one of the twins staring up at her.

"Sean — !" she cried. "You scared me! I — "

"I'm Seth," he said softly. "I'm sorry, Jenny. I thought you heard me."

He appeared so small, so pale, in the dim hall light. His pajama sleeves hung down over his hands.

"I — I was just going to check out the attic," Jenny told him shakily, still struggling to catch her breath.

"No, you can't," he replied, his voice just above a whisper.

Jenny stared down at him in surprise. "Huh? Why not?"

"It's locked," he told her. He grabbed the glass knob and turned it. "See? Mom keeps it locked. No one is allowed to go up there."

Jenny tried the door, too. Seth was right. The door was locked.

"But why?" she asked him.

"It's too dangerous," Seth replied quickly. He scratched his thick, blond hair.

Creeeeeak . . . creeeeak.

Jenny gasped. The footsteps sounded so near.

She raised her eyes to the ceiling.

"It's okay," Seth said. He didn't appear at all frightened or concerned.

Jenny turned back to him. "Too dangerous? Seth — what do you mean?"

He shrugged his slender shoulders. "I think the stairs are broken or something. Or maybe the attic floor. Mom said it was too dangerous. So she locked the door."

How weird, Jenny thought, glancing back up to the creaking ceiling.

Or maybe it wasn't weird at all. Maybe the attic stairs really were in bad repair. The Warsaws had just moved in a few weeks before. Mrs. Warsaw wouldn't have had time to have them fixed.

Creeeeeak.

Jenny decided to ignore the creaks and groans. Seth wasn't the least bit afraid of them. So why should she be afraid?

"Let me tuck you in again," she said softly. She placed a hand on his shoulder and guided him back to his room. "Hey, Seth — where's your dad?" The question blurted out. Since she had met the family, Jenny had been wondering where Mr. Warsaw was.

"He died," Seth replied, without any emotion at all.

"Oh. I'm sorry," Jenny said. She shook her head. *Why did I ask that question now? Why do these things pop into my head?*

Seth climbed back up to the top bunk. *Sean must already be asleep,* Jenny told herself. He didn't stir. "Good night, Seth," she whispered. "Sweet dreams."

She saw him pull the blanket up to his head. "Night, Jenny." A tiny whisper. Like a mouse squeak.

Ignoring the sounds from the attic, Jenny made her way downstairs. She pulled a diet Coke from the refrigerator, then settled into the living room armchair to read the book she had brought.

After a few paragraphs, the words blurred on the page. *I'm not in the mood,* she decided.

She shut the book and dropped it to the floor.

She took a long sip from the soda can, listening for the creaking sounds. But she couldn't hear them from downstairs.

The phone rang. She set down the soda can and picked up the receiver. "Hello. Warsaws'."

"Jenny?"

"Oh, hi, Claire." Jenny felt glad to hear her friend's voice.

"Your mom said you were baby-sitting next door," Claire said. "She gave me the number. How's it going?"

"Okay. Good!" Jenny declared. "No problem."

"Does it feel kind of weird to be baby-sitting again?" Claire asked.

"Kind of," Jenny replied. "But I'm okay. Really. The kids are pretty good. They're all in bed."

"So you have time to talk?" Claire asked. "I heard some great gossip today. About Ashley Franklin and Gary Wilson."

Jenny chuckled. "Spill."

She and Claire talked and gossiped for nearly half an hour. The relaxed conversation made Jenny feel good.

I'm back to normal, she thought. Back to a

normal life. Back to myself again.

Then, a few minutes later, the phone rang again.

And Jenny heard the voice she hoped never to hear again.

The whispered, raspy voice that had filled her life with so much horror.

"Hi, Jenny," he whispered. *"Hi, Jenny — it's me."*

Chapter 11

A low moan escaped Jenny's throat.

She gripped the phone so hard, her hand ached.

Mr. Hagen is dead, she reminded herself. He can't be calling me.

He can't.

The frightening phone calls had been the beginning of Jenny's troubles. Two nights a week, she had baby-sat for the Hagens' little boy. But then the whispered calls started: *"Company's coming, Babes."*

Calls from Mr. Hagen. He was crazy. He hated baby-sitters. All baby-sitters. He called Jenny again and again. Frightening, whispered calls.

And now she heard the terrifying whisper again in her ear.

"Hi, Jenny. It's me."

"Who — who is this?" Jenny demanded.

"It's me. Cal."

"Huh?" She nearly dropped the phone. "Cal? You — you scared me," she stammered. "Why are you whispering like that?"

"I can barely talk," Cal rasped. "Laryngitis. I have the *worst* sore throat."

Jenny let out a long, relieved sigh. She slumped back in the armchair. "I — I thought — "

"How's it going?" Cal whispered.

Jenny had to laugh. "It was going okay till you called. That scary whisper — it really frightened me."

"Sorry," Cal replied. "I always get bad sore throats like this. Listen, let me come over and make it up to you."

"I don't think so," Jenny replied. She wrapped the phone cord around her wrist, then unwrapped it.

"I won't stay long," he told her. "Half an hour. Then I'll go. Promise."

"It's not a good idea," Jenny replied.

"It's an excellent idea," he whispered.

"You're sick — remember? You shouldn't go out."

"I'm not sick," Cal protested. "I just have laryngitis." He suddenly sounded hurt. "Don't you *want* to see me?"

"Of course I want to see you," Jenny replied.

"Then why can't I come over there?"

She giggled. "Because you're bad."

"Who? Me?"

"You're bad," she repeated, teasing him. "You won't leave after half an hour. Mrs. Warsaw will come back home and find you here."

"No way!" he protested.

"Give me a break, Cal," Jenny said, turning serious. "This is my first night baby-sitting here. You know I can really use the money. I don't want to blow this job."

"But, Jen — " he started.

"No, Cal. N-O."

"Does that mean yes?"

She started to laugh. But a sudden chill made her stop.

A cold presence in the room. As if someone had suddenly turned the air conditioner on high.

And then Jenny felt fingers around her neck. Cold, bony fingers. From behind her.

So cold. So cold and wet.

Tightening. Tightening around her neck.

With a gasp, she dropped the phone receiver.

Then she started to scream.

"Jenny — what is it? What's happening?" She could hear Cal's raspy voice from the phone receiver on the floor.

Jenny leaped up. Spun around.

No one there. No one.

The grip of cold still tingling her neck.

She rubbed her neck with both hands, smoothing away the cold, rubbing away the feeling of bony fingers.

"Jenny — are you okay?" Cal's urgent cries from the phone at her feet. "Jenny? Answer me!"

Breathing hard, she swung herself around to the back of the big armchair.

"Who's hiding back there? Who grabbed my neck?"

No one back there.

"Who's trying to scare me?" she called, moving around the small room, searching behind the couch, examining the stairway in the front hall.

No one.

The cold lingered heavily in the room. The tingling at the back of her neck faded slowly.

Who *was* it? How did they disappear so quickly?

Shaking her head, she bent and picked up

the phone. "It's okay," she said breathlessly. "I'm okay."

"What happened?" Cal demanded, his voice even more of a hoarse croak. "I heard you scream."

"I . . . well . . ."

She didn't want to tell him. What could she say? That the room suddenly got cold and an invisible hand had grabbed her neck and started to strangle her?

If she told him that, Cal would have no choice. He would have to call Jenny's mother and tell her that Jenny was cracking up again.

"I . . . just dropped my soda can," she lied. "Call you later — okay? I'd better mop up the rug."

"Are you sure — ?" Cal started.

"Call you later." She hung up the phone.

She leaned her head against the armchair back, catching her breath.

I'm okay, she told herself. I'm perfectly okay.

She glanced around the room again. Everything in place. Everything okay.

She stood up slowly. Checked behind the chair one more time.

It's the boys, she decided. Sean and Seth. Playing a joke on me. Trying to scare me to death.

She started toward the stairs. Probably Sean, she told herself. There's something mean-natured about that one. Seth is so sweet. But Sean definitely has a cruel streak.

She thought about how mean Sean was to his sister. He was constantly teasing Meredith and doing things to show her he was boss.

Both boys look so angelic, Jenny thought with a smile. With that white-blond hair, the serious brown eyes, the pale white skin. Like perfect angels.

It's funny how two brothers can look so totally alike, Jenny thought, but still have such different personalities.

Grabbing the iron banister, she pulled herself up the stairs. I've got to tell them no more mean tricks, she told herself.

I've got to be firm with them right from the start.

No more scaring the baby-sitter. From now on, bedtime is bedtime. If I get the rules straight now, I won't have any trouble with them later.

She reached the second-floor landing, turned into the narrow hall, and strode quickly to the twins' room.

The door was closed.

That's weird, Jenny thought. After I tucked

Seth in for the second time, I remember leaving the door open.

She grabbed the handle and pushed open the door.

"Hey, guys — "

Even in the dim light from the hall, Jenny could see that they were gone.

Chapter 12

With a trembling hand, she groped along the wall until she found the lightswitch. She clicked on the ceiling light.

The blankets on the bunk beds were tossed back. One pillow lay on the carpet.

"Seth? Sean?" Jenny called weakly. Her eyes frantically darted around the room.

She dropped to all fours and peered under the bed.

No. They weren't hiding under there.

She climbed to her feet, crossed the small room, and pulled open the closet door.

Not in there, either.

"Hey — where are you two hiding?" she called. "This isn't funny, you know."

Silence.

"Come on, guys. You're scaring me!" Jenny called. "This isn't a funny joke."

She pulled up the blankets on both beds to

make sure they weren't hiding beneath them. Then she bent down to peer under the small desk.

Not there.

Nowhere else to search in the bedroom.

She returned to the door. "Seth? Sean?"

When she heard soft giggling out in the hall, Jenny breathed a long sigh of relief. "Hey, you two — !" She strode quickly into the hallway.

More giggling. From behind a partly open door at the end of the hall.

Jenny jogged toward the sound of soft laughter. Pulled open the door. A clothes closet. Both boys peered up at her from deep in the closet. Wide grins on their faces.

"Not funny!" Jenny scolded. She reached in and pulled them out, one hand for each. They didn't resist. "Not funny!" she repeated.

They both laughed harder. "Yes, it was!" they cried in unison. They flashed each other glances and started laughing again.

Jenny dragged them out into the center of the hallway. "Listen to me, guys," she insisted. "Do you want me to come baby-sit for you again?"

"Yes," Seth replied. Sean nodded.

"Then don't scare me anymore. I really mean it."

"Why not?" Sean demanded, his eyes

gleaming mischievously. "It was just a joke."

"I don't like those kind of jokes," Jenny replied sternly. "They get me really upset."

Their grins faded. Jenny could see that she was finally getting through to them. "Now let me tuck you in," she said, softening her tone. "But from now on, when I tuck you in, you have to stay tucked in. Okay?"

They muttered agreement.

The ceiling creaked.

Jenny automatically glanced up. The boys didn't pay any attention. "Did you hear that?" she blurted out.

Sean nodded. "There's someone locked up there," he told Jenny. "A prisoner."

He grinned at Seth. Seth gave him a playful shove. Both boys uttered high-pitched giggles.

"Ha-ha. Funny joke," Jenny said sarcastically. "You guys are real funny tonight."

The ceiling creaked again. This time Jenny ignored it. She guided the boys to their room and tucked them into the bunk beds. She said good night again and clicked off the ceiling light.

Now maybe they'll go to sleep, she told herself.

She started down the stairs. But stopped a third of the way down.

She heard footsteps in the living room.

A loud crash. Glass shattering on the floor.
More footsteps. Coming closer.
Jenny gripped the iron banister.
Someone has broken in, she realized.
Now what do I do?

Chapter 13

She didn't have time to do anything.

A shadow fell over the stairway. And then a tall figure stepped out of the living room.

"Huh? You?" she shrieked.

Cal raised his eyes to her. "Oh, wow! Thank goodness!" he cried in his hoarse voice. He flew up the stairs and wrapped his arms around her.

"Cal? What are you doing here?" Jenny cried breathlessly. "You — you scared me to death. I thought — "

He placed two fingers on her lips. Then, still holding her tightly, he lowered his head and kissed her.

A short kiss. Jenny pulled back quickly, eager to get some answers. "I told you *not* to come here," she said shrilly. "And then you break in, and — "

"I didn't break in," Cal replied in a raspy whisper. They both sat down on the bottom step. "The door was open a little, so I let myself in."

"But what are you *doing* here?" Jenny repeated impatiently.

"You screamed," Cal replied, taking her hand. "When I was talking to you on the phone. You sounded so frightened. I knew it wasn't just a soda can dropping. So I drove over as fast as I could."

"Cal — I really can take care of myself," Jenny replied angrily. "I know you think I'm still a total basket case. But, really — "

"That's *not* what I think!" Cal cried. He let go of her hand and jumped to his feet. "I know you're okay now, Jen. But when you screamed like that, I thought — "

"Okay, okay," Jenny replied, motioning for him to sit back down beside her. "You're right. I didn't drop a soda can. I heard something, and it startled me — okay? Big deal. That was no reason for you to come running over here and — "

"Didn't you hear me ringing the bell?" Cal demanded. "I rang and rang, and you didn't answer. So I got even more worried."

"I didn't hear it," Jenny told him. "The bell must be broken. The Warsaws just moved in.

They haven't had time to fix things up."

"When you didn't come to the door, I tried it, and it was open," Cal continued. "So I let myself in. When I saw you weren't in the living room, I started to get really scared. I started searching the house."

"I heard a crash," Jenny said. "I thought — "

"I was a little crazed," Cal admitted. "I walked right into the coffee table. I'm afraid I broke a glass vase. I — I'll help you clean it up."

"You always were a total klutz," Jenny teased. She was starting to feel better. It was nice to know that Cal cared about her enough to drop everything and come running to her like that.

He's really a great guy, she thought.

She pulled down his head with both hands and kissed him long and tenderly. As his lips moved against hers, he slid his arms around her waist and held her tight.

I feel so safe when Cal is around, Jenny thought.

But she scolded herself for thinking it. I have to feel completely safe when *I'm* the only one around, she told herself. I don't need someone else to make me feel safe.

When the kiss ended, Jenny took a moment to catch her breath. She ruffled Cal's white-blond hair. Then she grabbed both of his hands and tugged him to his feet.

They cleaned up the broken vase. Then she dragged him to the front door. "You're outta here!" she exclaimed, giving him a playful shove.

"Just a few more minutes," he pleaded, cupping his hands in a prayer position.

Jenny glanced at the clock. Just past ten-thirty.

"No way. Beat it," she insisted, giving him another shove. "Mrs. Warsaw will be home any second."

"Okay, okay," Cal grumbled. He turned at the front door. His smile faded. "You still didn't tell me why you screamed."

"Oh . . . well . . ." Jenny hesitated. She didn't want to tell him about the cold fingers on the back of her neck. She didn't want to tell him what a frightening night she'd been having before he arrived.

She shrugged. "It's just been a crazy night," she said, trying to sound light and unconcerned. "You know. Weird noises in the attic. Weird noises downstairs." She grinned at him. "A weirdo coming to visit . . ."

He smiled, but she caught his eyes staring hard at her, studying her. "You sure you're okay?"

"Cal — give me a break!" she exclaimed, pressing both hands against her waist. "Of *course* I'm okay. My house is right next door. What on earth could happen to me here?"

The phone rang about ten minutes after Cal left. Jenny had been watching TV, channel-surfing, not really paying attention to anything on the screen.

When the phone rang, she clicked off the TV. She picked up the receiver after the second ring. "Hello?"

"Hi, Jenny. It's me." Mrs. Warsaw. Jenny could hear a lot of voices in the background. People laughing. "How's it going?" Mrs. Warsaw asked, shouting over the noise.

"Fine," Jenny told her. "Just fine. The kids are asleep."

"Oh, that's great," Mrs. Warsaw replied, sounding relieved. "They usually give their baby-sitter a hard time about bedtime."

"Well, Sean and Seth were a little difficult," Jenny confessed.

"What? I'm sorry," Mrs. Warsaw shouted. "It's so noisy here. I couldn't hear you, Jenny. What about Sean?"

"Nothing. Not important," Jenny assured her. "Everything is fine."

"Well, I'm just calling to say I'll be a little

later than I thought. I should be home by eleven-thirty. That isn't a problem — is it, dear?"

"No. No problem," Jenny replied, glancing at the brass clock on the mantel.

Mrs. Warsaw shouted good-bye. Jenny heard a burst of loud laughter behind her. The line went dead.

Sounds like a good party, Jenny thought, hanging up the phone. She wondered if it was too late to call Claire.

Maybe I'd better not, she decided. Claire's dad is a light sleeper. He always gets furious if anyone calls after ten.

Jenny climbed to her feet and stretched. She walked around the room, examining the bookshelves, picking up glass and china knick-knacks.

Mrs. Warsaw seemed to have a collection of little glass animals. Jenny picked up a tiny tiger, then a tiny monkey with a curled-up tail. She rubbed her finger against the glass. So smooth.

I hope that glass vase Cal broke wasn't important to Mrs. Warsaw, Jenny thought, frowning. I hope it wasn't part of a priceless vase collection or something.

She started to pick up a china mermaid. The figurine had long, shiny red hair that rolled like an ocean wave down the length of her body to her emerald-green tail fin.

But Jenny stopped her hand in midair as she felt another wave of cold descend over the room.

She spun away from the display shelf.

No one there.

Maybe the air-conditioning clicked on, she thought. But she heard no hum. She saw no air-conditioning vent.

The cold pressed down on her, damp, clammy, heavy. She suddenly felt as if she were underwater, under a heavy, cold wave.

And then she heard a whispered voice, so close, so close to her ear:

"Go away, Jenny."

"Huh?" Jenny uttered a startled cry. Her eyes squinted over the small room. "Who's there?"

"Go away, Jenny," the whispery voice repeated. *"Go away. Or you'll die, too."*

Chapter 14

"Who — who's there?" Jenny stammered.

She ran to the hallway, frantically peering both ways.

No one.

"Seth? Sean?" she called.

The whispered voice was so close. The room felt so cold.

As if she had stepped into a refrigerator.

"Who said that?" Jenny cried, running to the living room window and staring out into the darkness. Then diving to the floor and searching beneath the couch, beneath the armchair.

Where? Where? Where?

She knew the answer. But she didn't want to admit it.

She knew who was whispering to her. Knew where the voice was coming from.

Coming from inside her.

Coming from inside her own head.

"No! No way!" she cried out loud.

I'm not freaking out again! she told herself.
I'm not crazy!

I'm not going back to the hospital — ever
again. I'm normal now, she thought, gritting
her teeth, concentrating, concentrating. Trying to drive the voice away, so far away it
would never come back.

I can control it, Jenny thought. Because I'm
not crazy. I'm not.

*"Go away, Jenny. Go away. Or you'll die,
too."*

What did that mean? I'll die, *too*?

Jenny shut her eyes. She pressed her hands
against her temples.

Go away, voice. Go away.

I can will you away. I can force you away.

I am normal, normal, *normal*!

A face flashed into Jenny's thoughts. Becka.
A girl she knew in the hospital. A pretty,
cheerful girl with sleek, straight black hair
down to her shoulders, and cold green eyes.

Becka had been ready to go home, Jenny
remembered. After a long stay at the hospital,
Becka had impressed the doctors enough to
send her home to her parents.

Becka was a few years younger than Jenny.
They had started a conversation one afternoon
in the TV room. Neither of them was inter-

ested in the game shows on the TV every afternoon. So they found themselves talking, about their schools, about their families, about boys.

Most of the time, Becka was cheerful and talkative. Jenny couldn't tell why her new friend had been sent to the hospital. Whenever she brought up the subject, Becka shrugged and muttered that it was a long story.

Becka obviously didn't want to talk about it. Jenny didn't press her.

Because Jenny didn't really feel like talking about her troubles, either. About the voices she heard, the voices telling her that she was Mr. Hagen. That she was no longer Jenny. That she was now Mr. Hagen back from the grave.

And so they avoided the most important subject in their lives. And talked about movies and books they liked, vacations they had been on, normal things.

It was so important to be normal. Such an important goal.

Of course, Becka had her moody days. Her days when her green eyes lost their sparkle and she seemed to sink into herself, deep into herself. So deep that Jenny couldn't reach her.

Such a scary feeling. To be talking to someone and suddenly realize that, even though she's still sitting beside you, she's no longer there.

But the moody days grew fewer and farther apart. And then Becka seemed to be cheerful and alert whenever Jenny saw her. "I've got to get out of here," she confided to Jenny. "I'll do anything. If I spend another month in this hospital, I'll *really* crack up."

And one sunny October day, the doctors decided that Becka was normal and healthy again. What a happy day that had been.

When Becka told her the news that they were sending her home, Jenny had been so glad for her. Glad — and unhappy that she was about to lose a friend.

A few days later, Jenny crossed the hall into Becka's room to say good-bye. Becka's little sister had sent Becka a soft, brown teddy bear. On her bad days, Becka had clung to the bear, holding it tightly against her chest, refusing to let it go, even at mealtimes.

Now Jenny found Becka sitting on top of the bedcovers, in jeans and a bright pink pullover — finally out of her pale gray hospital gown.

The teddy bear rested in her lap.

Becka had ripped the head off the bear.

As Jenny stared in horror, Becka kept dipping her hand inside the bear's body, pulling out big chunks of white cotton stuffing, and eating them.

Becka still wasn't normal.

The doctors were ready to send her home. But Becka still had problems.

Standing in the middle of Mrs. Warsaw's living room, Jenny shook her head, trying to shake away her painful memories of Becka.

I'm not ready yet, either, she told herself, feeling the bitter tears brim in her eyes.

I'm just like Becka. I'm still messed up.

I'm still hearing voices. Threatening voices inside my head.

Why did the doctors let me come home? They told me I'm ready — but I'm not! I'm not!

No.

Stop it, Jenny. Stop it.

Shut up, Jenny. Take a deep breath, she instructed herself.

She dropped into the armchair and shut her eyes.

Calm down. You can figure this out, she thought.

You're not crazy. You know you're not. You're not going to *let* yourself get crazy. You're going to keep it together — no matter what it takes.

Becka's face floated into her thoughts again. And once again, Jenny saw the headless teddy bear, saw Becka hungrily swallowing the cotton stuffing.

She opened her eyes and stood up.

I'm not Becka. I'm Jenny.

And I'm not crazy. I know where the voice is coming from.

An intercom, Jenny thought. Sometimes parents have an intercom to listen in on a child's room at night.

The twins are playing another trick on me. They're using an intercom in their room to whisper that frightening message.

But where is the speaker?

Jenny frantically searched the living room. Her eyes swept over the cluttered bookshelves, over the glass vases and china animal figurines. She searched the desktop, peered on the shelf under the coffee table.

When she couldn't find an intercom speaker, she ran up the stairs to the boys' bedroom. She clicked on a ceiling light in the hall. It cast pale yellow light into the narrow room.

The boys were asleep on their backs, their covers pulled up to their chins. In the lower bunk, Sean was snoring lightly.

Are they faking? Jenny wondered. Are they pretending to sleep?

She crossed the room to the bunk beds and examined their faces. "Are you awake?" she whispered.

Neither of them moved.

Jenny turned and searched the room once again, this time looking for an intercom. Silently, she searched every surface, every shelf, every possible hiding place. She even pulled out the drawers of the desk, carefully shuffling through the contents of each drawer.

No luck.

With a dispirited sigh, she crept out of the bedroom and clicked off the hall light. Nice try, Jenny, she thought bitterly. A nice theory. But there's no intercom.

The boys are asleep. Neither one was the whisperer.

Then who was?

She had just stepped back into the living room when the cold whisper rasped in her ears once again.

"Go away, Jenny. Go away NOW!"

So close.

The dry croak of a voice so close. She could feel the rush of cold, damp air on the back of her neck. Every muscle in her body tightened. Hard goosebumps rose up and down her arms.

"Where are you?" she choked out. "Who are you? Are you inside me? Are you inside my head?"

"Go away now, Jenny. Go away, or you'll die, too."

Chapter 15

"So you're not going to baby-sit anymore?" Claire asked.

Jenny shook her head. She felt embarrassed. She didn't really want to talk about it. "No. I don't think so."

"The kids were animals?" Claire asked.

"No. They were okay," Jenny replied. "It's kind of hard to explain. The house was . . . well . . . creepy."

"If you were uncomfortable there, you did the right thing," Claire said. "You shouldn't go somewhere you're uncomfortable."

Maybe I'll be uncomfortable wherever I go, Jenny thought bitterly.

"Hey, Jenny — your turn," Cal called from the bench.

"Are we going to talk, or are we going to bowl?" Rick chimed in.

"Both!" Claire called back to him.

Jenny hoisted up her bowling ball and stepped up to the lane. "Who's winning?" she called back.

"Cal is," Rick replied, glancing at the score sheet. "That's because he cheats."

"Huh? Cheat?" Cal cried in mock horror. "Give me a break! How can you cheat at bowling?"

"I can never figure out how to keep score," Claire said, pulling back her dark brown hair, fixing her ponytail. She wore an oversized white T-shirt over a sleeveless blue T-shirt and tight-fitting denim cutoffs that emphasized her long legs. "All those lines and X's."

"You don't have any X's!" Rick called, snickering. "All I see are two threes and a six!"

"At least I'm beating you!" Claire shot back.

"I have a sprained wrist," Rick replied, holding up a limp hand. "Otherwise, I'd be bowling a perfect game."

Cal motioned to Jenny. "Anytime tonight!" he called impatiently.

Jenny raised the ball to her waist and prepared to bowl. She hesitated. She could never remember whether to start her approach with her right foot or her left foot.

She took a deep breath and stepped forward. As she brought her arm forward to release the ball, it brushed the side of her jeans.

The ball bounced on to the lane, rolled straight for a few feet, then spun into the gutter.

"Not again!" she cried, raising both hands to the sides of her hair.

"Maybe you should aim for the gutter," Rick teased. "Then it might go down the alley."

"Maybe we should get that lane over there," Cal suggested, grinning. He pointed to the kiddie lane at the far side. It had bumpers down both sides so that the ball couldn't go into the gutter.

Rick laughed and slapped Cal a high five.

Claire raised her bowling ball toward the two boys. "You know, this would look really good in your mouth!" she cried.

Jenny's ball rolled back onto the rack, and she picked it up. She stepped up to the lane, made her approach, and let the ball go. This time she toppled all of the pins except for the tenpin.

"Yaaay!" She let out a cheer and clapped her hands. "Almost a spare!"

"It's called a nine," Rick said, sneering.

Laughing, Jenny stepped over to the scorers' table and gave him a hard shove. "You're a real beast, Rick," she muttered.

"But he's kind of cute," Claire chimed in.

Rick actually blushed.

Cal stepped up to take his turn. He was a

good bowler, Jenny saw. He took the game more seriously than the other three.

Of course, Jenny knew, Cal took most everything seriously. He didn't really like to kid around the way most of their friends did. He just didn't have the patience for it.

Rick left to get a Coke. Claire sat down beside Jenny at the scorers' table. "So are you okay?" she asked, her dark eyes probing Jenny's.

"Huh? What do you mean?" Jenny replied, confused.

"I mean, about the baby-sitting thing last night," Claire explained. She pulled a string off the shoulder of Jenny's blue-and-white striped tank top. "What happened when that woman came home? Mrs. . . . ?"

"Warsaw," Jenny said.

"Did you tell her you wouldn't baby-sit any-more?" Claire asked.

Jenny shook her head. "No. Not really. It was kind of late. And I just wanted to get home."

I wanted to get away from the cold, whispering voice, Jenny thought unhappily. But how can I get away from it if it's inside my head?

"So you just told her everything was fine?" Claire continued.

"Yeah. Pretty much," Jenny said, watching Cal topple every pin except the lead pin. He scowled and tugged at his white-blond hair.

"I told her the kids were very good," Jenny said. "I said everything went okay." She sighed. "I mean, what's the point of starting a big thing? I just felt uncomfortable in the house. It kind of creeped me out. No big deal."

"Right," Claire agreed, motioning with both hands for Jenny to calm down. "You're definitely right."

Jenny hadn't realized she was shouting. She could feel her face grow hot.

Take it easy, Jenny, she warned herself. You don't want Claire to start thinking you're still a nut case.

Cal knocked the one pin down with his second ball, making his spare. "Yes!" he cried triumphantly. He flashed Jenny a smile.

Claire leaned close to Jenny. "If you do decide to go back there . . . you know . . . to baby-sit, I'll be happy to go along with you," she said quietly. "It would be kind of fun, don't you think?"

"Thanks, Claire," Jenny replied, feeling very embarrassed.

"And if you ever need to talk . . ." Claire continued, staring hard into Jenny's eyes.

"Thanks," Jenny repeated.

Claire is trying to be a good friend, Jenny told herself. But she's trying too hard.

I shouldn't have mentioned that I got a little freaked out last night. I shouldn't have mentioned that I decided not to baby-sit for Mrs. Warsaw again.

Now Claire keeps examining me like I'm some kind of lab specimen.

"It's your turn," she told Claire. "Let's see if we can beat these guys."

Cal pulled his face away. The taste of his lips lingered on hers.

Jenny pressed her forehead against his shoulder. "I had fun tonight," she said softly.

"Me, too," Cal replied. He turned from the steering wheel and shifted his arm around her. He lifted her chin with one finger and kissed her again.

When I'm with Cal, I'm okay, Jenny thought dreamily.

Cal had pulled his car halfway up her driveway and cut the headlights. The house was dark. Jenny knew her mom went to bed pretty early on work nights.

She snuggled against Cal. "You're a pretty awesome bowler," she told him.

He snickered. "I didn't have much competition tonight."

"Poor Rick!" Jenny exclaimed. "When he dropped the ball on his foot — "

"He just did that so he won't have to go to work tomorrow!" Cal interrupted.

Jenny smiled. "He hates his summer job so much."

"Why doesn't he just quit?" Cal demanded.

"He doesn't want to hurt his uncle's feelings. His uncle thinks that Rick *loves* the job. He wants to send Rick to shoe college or something!"

They both giggled.

"Rick should just quit," Cal insisted.

Jenny poked him in the ribs. "Look who's talking. You don't exactly love your job at the garage — do you?"

Cal frowned. "It's okay," he insisted. "I like messing with cars, you know. And the money isn't too bad."

Jenny saw that she had hit a sore spot. Cal didn't like to be reminded about some things. She pulled his head down and kissed him. That was the best way to get the frown off his face.

They stayed in the driveway for another half hour, talking softly, snuggling together. This is the nicest night I've had since I left the hospital, Jenny thought happily. It's the first night I've really felt relaxed.

It was nearly one in the morning when she

climbed out of Cal's car and made her way into the house. She felt sleepy and alert, relaxed and excited — all at the same time.

She turned at the door and watched Cal's car back down the driveway. He flashed on the headlights when he reached the street, then sped away.

Jenny could still taste his kisses, still feel the warmth of his arms around her. She closed the front door carefully, silently, not wanting to awaken her mother. Then she crept upstairs to her room.

She fumbled around in the darkness until she managed to click on the lamp on her bed table. Blinking as her eyes adjusted to the light, she saw a sheet of lined paper on her pillow.

A note from her mother. Jenny scooped it up and read it quickly:

How are you? Do I ever get to see you? Or shall we just send notes? Good night. Love, Mom.

Jenny smiled.

Constant communication. That's what her mom liked. She believed in keeping in touch all day long.

Yawning, Jenny pulled off her tank top and

jeans, leaving them in a heap on the bedroom carpet. She pulled a filmy short nightshirt from her dresser drawer and slipped it on.

The room felt hot. Jenny turned to the window and saw that it was shut. "I need some fresh air," she murmured out loud.

She crossed the room to the window and peered out. Pale moonlight washed over the backyard, making the lawn glisten.

Jenny's eyes followed the light to the Warsaws' house next door. She reached to pull open the window — then stopped.

What was that near the Warsaws' roof?

Moonlight filled the attic window.

Something moved in the silvery light.

A face. A girl's face, her dark eyes reflecting the light.

Sad eyes. A sad face.

Jenny pressed against the windowpane, staring hard.

Am I seeing things? Am I hallucinating?

No.

Jenny hurriedly pulled up the window. Pushed up the screen. And stuck her head out.

She could see the girl's face so clearly now. Dark eyes. A full, red mouth. The pretty face framed by black curls.

The girl stared out the window, stared right at Jenny.

And what were the words she was mouthing?

Jenny struggled to read the girl's lips. What was she saying?

It looked like: "Help me. Help me."

Chapter 16

"Help me. Help me!"

Were those her words?

Jenny leaned farther out the window, struggling to see.

The backyard suddenly darkened. A cloud rolled over the moon. The dark shadow swept over the lawn, onto the Warsaws' house.

The attic window darkened to black.

The girl's face faded with it.

Jenny waited for the light to return. Down the block, she heard a car door slam. A dog barked. A gust of wind fluttered her hair.

A few seconds later, the cloud silently rolled away. The light washed over the yard, over the house next door. Filled the attic window.

But the face had vanished.

Jenny shivered, suddenly chilled. The night air was warm. But the silvery light felt so cold.

She gazed out at the empty attic window.

Waited for the sad-eyed girl to return.

Waited and watched.

Who are you, girl? Jenny wondered. Just a picture in my mind?

A face in my imagination?

No, Jenny thought. No. There's something strange at Mrs. Warsaw's house. Something strange and frightening over there.

Jenny gazed at the house through the cold, silver moonlight.

The window glowed, reflecting the light.

The girl didn't appear again.

Jenny pulled herself back into the room and went to bed.

She had a nightmare. The first one in several months.

The dream started out pleasantly. Jenny found herself in a bowling alley. She saw herself bowling easily, gracefully.

The pins toppled with a pleasant *clonk* of wood against wood.

Rick applauded. Jenny took a bow.

She bowled again. The ball felt so light. Jenny felt so light. She floated across the lane.

The pins fell, silently this time.

A boy appeared. Was it Cal?

Yes. Cal smiled at her. He lifted a bag. A green bowling bag.

"Is that yours?" Jenny asked.

Cal nodded with a grin. "Guess what's inside," he urged.

Jenny stared at the bowling bag. "What's inside?" she asked.

"Guess," Cal insisted stubbornly.

Jenny pulled the bag from Cal's hands. It wasn't as heavy as she'd imagined. In fact, it felt light, light as a feather.

"Guess what's inside," Cal repeated.

Jenny unzipped the bag. She pulled it open and peered inside.

A head stared up at her.

Claire's head.

Claire's head was in the bowling bag.

The head opened its eyes. Then its mouth twisted open, and it began to howl. A hideous animal howl.

Jenny held the bowling bag in both hands, and she began to howl, too. Jenny howled, and Claire's head howled.

Jenny awoke and sat straight up in bed.

The dream lingered. The howling didn't stop.

She pressed her hands against her ears. "What a weird dream!" she uttered.

But why didn't the howling stop?

Lowering her hands, she slowly realized the howls came from outside.

She lowered herself shakily to her feet. The strange cries seemed to come from nearby, from the backyard.

The ugly dream stayed with her as she made her way to the window. What on earth does it mean? she wondered, blinking hard, trying to force it to leave her mind.

And who is making those awful wails?

She pushed aside the curtains. Poked her head out the window.

Caught a glimpse of a blond-haired boy. Darting across the backyard.

"Sean? Is that you?" her sleep-choked voice didn't carry far. "Sean? Seth?"

The howls faded. The boy vanished.

Jenny stared down at the backyard, shivering.

What is going on? What is happening?

Half-awake, half in her dream, she stared out into the now-silent night, wondering what was real — and what wasn't.

She pulled herself up when she heard the sound behind her.

A floorboard creak. A footstep.

Someone is in my bedroom, Jenny realized.

Chapter 17

Shivering, Jenny spun around.

Someone moved by the doorway.

The curtains wrapped around Jenny, tangled over her, clouding her view. With a low cry, she frantically pulled them away.

"Mom!" she whispered.

Mrs. Jeffers moved quickly toward Jenny. The moonlight revealed her worried expression. "What's wrong? I heard you walking around in here."

"I . . . uh . . . heard something," Jenny replied. She pointed to the window.

"Me, too," Mrs. Jeffers said softly.

Jenny let out a long sigh of relief. I didn't imagine it, she thought happily. Even Mom, who can sleep through anything, heard the howls, too.

"There's been a prowler in the neighborhood," her mom reported. "I didn't tell you. I didn't want to worry you. I mean — "

Jenny moved away from the window. "A prowler?"

"He doesn't steal anything," Mrs. Jeffers said. "He just does mischief. You know. Vandalism. He tips over garbage cans. Breaks windows. Cuts up lawn furniture. It happened at the Miller house two nights ago. They found their mailbox at the bottom of their swimming pool."

"Weird," Jenny commented. She dropped down onto the edge of the bed.

Mrs. Jeffers jammed her hands into the pockets of her bathrobe. She looked older to Jenny in the silvery light. The lines around her eyes seemed deeper. Her skin appeared pale and dry.

"I thought I saw a boy," Jenny said hesitantly.

"Huh? A boy?"

"Yeah. Running across the backyard," Jenny told her. "He had blond hair. Like . . . like next door."

Mrs. Jeffers chewed her bottom lip. "Maybe we should call the police."

Jenny shrugged. "It's quiet out there now."

Her mother crossed to the window and peered down. A few seconds later, she turned back into the room. "Such bright moonlight," she murmured. "I don't see anyone. Let's get back to sleep, okay?"

Jenny nodded. She slid under the covers.

Mrs. Jeffers bent over her, kissed her on the forehead, the way she did when Jenny was a little girl. "Sweet dreams."

"Good night, Mom," Jenny whispered.

As she shut her eyes, she pictured the sad-eyed girl in the attic window. Then the blond-haired boy racing across the backyard.

Something strange at the Warsaws', Jenny thought sleepily.

Something strange next door . . .

Her last thought before falling back to sleep.

Jenny pulled open the dishwasher door. "I'll take care of the dishes, Mom," she said. "I know you're in a hurry."

Mrs. Jeffers had a date with Winston. She carried two plates to the counter, a fretful expression on her face. "I'm forty-three years old," she moaned. "I shouldn't be worrying about what to wear on a date."

Jenny laughed. "It's good for you. You seem so much happier, Mom."

Mrs. Jeffers shook her head. "Happy? I'm not sure. Nervous? Definitely." She picked up the dish towel and started to wipe at a stain near the sink.

"Mom — go get dressed. I'll take care of it," Jenny insisted.

Mrs. Jeffers turned and headed out of the kitchen. "Are you seeing Cal tonight?" she called back.

"No," Jenny told her. "He's working the late shift at the garage."

"I have to get gas in my car," Mrs. Jeffers said. "I'll tell him you say hi."

Ten minutes later, Jenny's mom was dressed and out the door. Watching her speed away, Jenny had to smile. Her mom certainly had been acting like a lovesick teenager.

Jenny had just finished loading the dishwasher and wiping the counter clean when she heard a knock at the kitchen door. She turned as Mrs. Warsaw stepped into the room.

"Jenny — are you busy?" she asked breathlessly. Her face was flushed. She had beads of sweat on her wide forehead.

Jenny hesitated. "Busy?"

"Can you come stay with the kids? Just for a few hours?"

"Well . . ." Jenny started. "I don't — "

"My sister was taken ill," Mrs. Warsaw interrupted. "They took her to County General. They don't really know what's wrong. I know this is short notice. But I'm really worried about her. I can't take the kids with me, so . . ." Her voice trailed off. Her eyes pleaded with Jenny.

"Of course I'll stay with them," Jenny replied. "I'm not doing anything tonight."

"Oh, thank you! Thank you!" Mrs. Warsaw gushed. "You're a doll. You really are."

"I'll just grab my keys and come back with you," Jenny said.

"This is so nice of you," Mrs. Warsaw said, wiping her forehead with a chubby hand. "I'll pay you double, Jenny. I really will."

"That isn't necessary," Jenny called from the front hallway.

"My poor sister. She doesn't get a break," Mrs. Warsaw continued. "First Al died. Then, Clarice got sick. Now this."

Mrs. Warsaw kept talking, but Jenny couldn't hear her. She pulled her house keys from the bowl on the hall table. Then she checked herself out in the mirror on the wall by the front door.

Her hair was a total mess. She had put it up to keep it off her shoulders, and half of it had come loose. But she guessed it really didn't matter.

Poor Mrs. Warsaw, Jenny thought. She seems to be in such a panic.

I have to help her out, Jenny told herself. I really have no choice. I have to put my fears aside. At least for tonight. It's an emergency, after all.

I'm sure everything will be fine tonight, Jenny assured herself. Perfectly fine.

Sean and Meredith were playing a video game in the living room. Jenny greeted them warmly. They grunted hello, but didn't turn away from the fighting figures on the TV screen.

Mrs. Warsaw was nearly out the front door when she dropped her purse. The contents clattered to the floor, coins rolling away, a lipstick tube bouncing under the couch.

Jenny helped the frazzled woman stuff everything back in the bag. "I hope your sister is okay," she said. "Don't worry about the kids. We'll be fine here."

"I gave them dinner," Mrs. Warsaw replied, searching for her car keys. "But they may want dessert later. There's a cake in a box on the counter. Be sure to help yourself, Jenny."

Mrs. Warsaw pushed open the screen door. "Be good, kids," she called back to them. "No fighting." She disappeared out the door.

Sean and Meredith didn't turn around.

"Die! Die, you scum!" Sean was screaming, frantically working the control pad.

"Where's Seth?" Jenny asked, dropping down onto the couch.

They didn't reply.

She was about to go searching for him when he walked into the room. He was wearing a sleeveless blue T-shirt and baggy blue shorts. "Hi, Jenny." He smiled at her. "I *thought* I heard you come in."

"Your mom had to go visit her sister," Jenny reported.

"I know," he replied, glancing at the noisy battle on the TV screen. "Hey, I get to play next!"

"When can we have cake?" Meredith demanded. Her first words to Jenny that evening.

"Yeah. We want cake!" Sean repeated.

All three began to chant: "We want cake! We want cake!"

"Okay, okay." Jenny jumped to her feet. "I'll go get it. But you'll have to come in the kitchen. You can't eat it in the living room."

Wow, she thought. Am I starting to sound like a parent or what?

Jenny found the white cake box on the kitchen counter. She cut the string with a pair of scissors, opened the lid, and carefully pulled out the cake.

"Mmmmm." She scooped a glob of chocolate frosting onto her finger and tasted it. Not bad. Maybe I'll have a slice, too, she decided.

She found a large cake knife in a wooden knife rack beside the toaster oven. Then she pulled down four small plates from the cabinet.

She was raising the heavy knife to slice the cake when she felt the sudden pressure on her arm.

"Hey — !" she cried out, startled.

She struggled to lower the knife. But something was pushing it, pushing it with great force. Something pushed her hand, pushed the knife away from the cake.

"Hey! What on earth — !"

Jenny struggled. But the invisible force overpowered her.

The wide blade gleamed in the bright kitchen light.

The knife turned in her hand.

"No!" she cried, trying to push the knife away, trying to get control of it.

The blade edged closer.

"No!"

She wasn't strong enough. Wasn't as strong as the invisible force.

She uttered a desperate cry.

And the blade plunged into her chest.

Chapter 18

"Noooo!"

Jenny stumbled back as the knife shot forward.

As the blade point started to pierce the front of her T-shirt, she dropped to the floor.

She landed hard. Pain shot up through her body.

She saw the knife sail over her shoulder, heard it clatter to the floor behind her.

She grabbed her chest.

I'm okay. I'm okay.

Breathing hard, her heart thumping, she pulled herself to a sitting position. She rubbed the front of her T-shirt, rubbed it until she was sure she wasn't cut.

And then she stared down at the knife.

"How — ?" she murmured out loud.

She turned to see the three kids in the

kitchen doorway, staring down at her in horror.

"Oh. Uh . . ." Had they seen the whole thing?

Had they seen her strange tug-of-war? Had they seen her nearly stab herself to death?

Seth was the first to move. "Jenny — what happened? Did you fall?" He came running over to help pull her to her feet.

Jenny sucked in a deep breath, tried to steady her trembling legs. They didn't see it, she decided. I can't tell them what happened. I don't want to frighten them.

And I don't want them to think I'm crazy.

"I — I slipped," she stammered. She leaned against the counter.

She turned to Sean, still in the doorway. He had a faint smile on his face. "Did you cut yourself?" he asked.

Jenny shook her head. "No. The knife just fell. I'm all right." She rubbed the front of her T-shirt, making sure one more time.

Why is Sean smiling like that? she wondered.

Seth carefully picked up the knife and handed it to her.

"Can we have our cake now?" Meredith demanded impatiently.

"Coming right up," Jenny replied, forcing a smile.

The kids enjoyed their cake. Meredith asked for seconds. The two boys hurried back to their video battle in front of the TV set.

Jenny felt too shaken to have a slice. She rinsed the cake knife off and examined it.

Nothing unusual.

A chill ran down her back. She felt confused and frightened. But she had to carry on, had to pretend that everything was okay. She didn't want to worry the kids.

The sink was piled high with dirty dishes from dinner. I'll load them in the dishwasher after I get the kids to bed, Jenny decided.

A short while later, Sean and Meredith got into a fight. Jenny wasn't even sure what it was about. She glanced up to see them wrestling on the living room carpet, screaming and flailing at each other.

She pulled them apart and took Meredith to bed. But Meredith was not in a cooperative mood. Jenny had to read her two Roald Dahl stories before she agreed to go to sleep.

When she finally returned to the living room, Jenny found the two boys watching a very adult movie on one of the cable movie channels.

After a ten-minute argument about why she couldn't allow them to watch that movie, she got them to agree to watching a tape. That led to another long argument about what tape to watch.

It was nearly eleven when she finally tucked the two boys into bed. She turned out their light and made her way down the hall.

She stopped at the attic door.

The face of the sad-eyed girl floated into her memory.

Jenny pressed her ear against the door and listened. Silence.

She tried the doorknob. It turned easily. But the door wouldn't pull open. It was locked.

She returned to the living room, feeling uneasy, wondering how late Mrs. Warsaw would be. She glanced at the clock on the mantel. Too late to call Claire.

Jenny swallowed hard. It would be nice to have some company, she thought. Cal was still at work. Her mother wasn't home yet.

She stepped into the kitchen and carried the dirty cake plates to the sink. Then she pulled open the dishwasher. I'll be better off if I keep busy, she told herself. She began rinsing off the dinner dishes and loading them into the dishwasher.

The job took only a few minutes. When the

dishes were all loaded, Jenny saw that the sink was filled with melon rinds and food scraps.

She shoved them into the drain. Found the switch for the garbage disposal and clicked it on.

It started up with a roar.

Water from the faucet flowed into the drain. The disposal made a deafening grinding sound as it began to devour the food scraps.

Jenny slid some more scraps toward the drain.

Then she felt the pressure on her hand.

Like an invisible hand, gripping hers, pushing it forward.

Pushing her hand toward the roaring drain.

Pushing her. Pushing her.

"No — !"

Jenny pushed back. Tried to leap back from the sink.

But the invisible force held her in place.

"Please — !" she screamed.

Straining, struggling, pulling back with all of her might, she watched her hand being forced into the grinding disposal blades.

Closer. Closer. The hot water spilling over the back of her hand. Her fingers disappearing into the drain now.

"Oh, please — !"

And then, in her terror, in her desperate

panic — a moment of clear thought.

With a frantic cry, she reached up her free hand — and clicked off the disposal.

The blades whirred to a stop. The roar faded to silence.

The invisible force vanished at once, leaving Jenny sobbing, leaning over the sink, her entire body trembling.

She sucked in breath after breath, trying to stop the shaking, the cold chills, the sobs from deep in her throat.

After a few seconds, she sensed that she wasn't alone.

She could feel someone close by, someone behind her.

Taking a deep breath, she spun around.

"Sean!" she choked out.

He stood inches away from her. His brown eyes stared up at her from under his tousled blond hair.

How long has he been standing here? Jenny wondered.

"Jenny — " he whispered, his eyes urgently locked on hers. "Jenny, I have to tell you something. Something very scary."

Chapter 19

"Huh?" Jenny stared down at him, struggling to think clearly. "Sean — what is it? What's the matter? Did you — ?"

"Jenny, please listen — " Sean urged in a whisper. He grabbed her arm. His hand felt so cold.

"What, Sean?" Jenny whispered back.

They both turned to the doorway as Seth strode into the room. "Can I have a glass of water?" he demanded. His eyes were on his twin brother.

Sean let go of Jenny's arm. He took a step back, his expression tight with fear.

"In a second," Jenny told Seth. She turned back to Sean. "What did you want to tell me, Sean? Go ahead. What is it?"

Sean hesitated. "Uh . . . I want water, too." He darted a glance at his brother.

Seth grinned at him.

"But you said — " Jenny started.

Sean shook his head. She saw his chin quiver. She could still see fear in his eyes. "No. Just water," Sean insisted. "I just came down for water."

"So Mrs. W got home after midnight?" Claire asked. She sat up and pulled a bottle of suntan lotion from her bag.

"Uh-huh," Jenny replied sleepily. "I was up almost all night. I couldn't get to sleep."

Claire rubbed a glob of the white lotion on her shoulders. Then she reached behind her and adjusted the back of her blue bikini top. "Want some?" She pushed the lotion bottle toward Jenny.

"No thanks." Jenny pushed her sunglasses up on her nose. "I want to burn for a while. The sun feels so good."

They had spread a blanket on the grassy lakeshore and were stretched out in their swimsuits, sunning and talking quietly. It was the next afternoon, a sultry, hot Saturday. The sun beamed down in a bright, cloudless sky. There was no wind at all. Not a leaf trembled on the trees behind the lakeshore.

Jenny needed to relax. And she needed to confide in someone.

What had happened at Mrs. Warsaw's house

was just too frightening. Jenny made Claire promise not to tell a soul. Then she told Claire the entire story.

Claire listened in silence, her dark eyes narrowed on the lake, her expression thoughtful.

Jenny told her about the girl in the window. About the strange howls at night. The blond boy running through the backyard. The whispered threats at Mrs. Warsaw's house. The cake knife. The garbage disposal.

When she finished, she waited for Claire to react.

But Claire stared back at her in silence for the longest time. Finally, she said softly, "Jenny, have you told this to Dr. Simonson?"

Jenny sat up on the blanket and uttered an angry cry. "You think I'm imagining it all — don't you, Claire!" she snapped angrily.

Claire didn't reply.

"You think I'm cracking up again!" Jenny accused. "Poor crazy Jenny — she's seeing things again. Is that what you think, Claire? Is it?" Jenny shrieked.

"Shhhh. Calm down," Claire replied softly. "I — I don't know what to think," she confessed. "I mean, the whole story — it's so . . . so . . ."

"So *crazy*?" Jenny finished the sentence for her.

"Come on, Jen — give me a break," Claire pleaded. "I'm trying to understand. But flying knives? Invisible hands shoving you into the disposal?"

"It happened!" Jenny insisted heatedly. "I didn't imagine it. It happened." Jenny uttered a sob. "You're my best friend, Claire. I thought that *you* would believe me."

"Okay, okay. I'm trying," Claire replied. "But you have to tell your psychiatrist, Jen. You have to tell her that — "

"I can't!" Jenny protested. "Don't you understand? She'll send me back to the hospital. But I'm not crazy. I'm not!"

Jenny grabbed Claire by the shoulders. Her hands slid over the greasy suntan oil. "You won't tell — will you? You won't tell anyone? You promised!"

Claire's eyes burned into Jenny's. "But what are you going to *do?*" she demanded.

"I'm going to prove that I'm not crazy," Jenny told her. "I'm going to prove that it all really happened. And I'm going to find out why."

When the howls rose up from the backyard late that night, Jenny was ready. She had stayed dressed. Had dozed in the chair beside her bedroom window.

The low animal wails made her jump to her feet, instantly alert. She leaned on the windowsill and peered down.

Into hazy swirls of fog.

Hot air fluttered her hair. She realized she was sweating.

The night felt as hot and humid as the day. A fog had descended around dinnertime, damp and gray. Now the moonlight shimmered off the fog clouds, making the backyard appear eerie. Unfamiliar.

Another howl rose up from the yard. And Jenny caught a glimpse of the little, blond-haired boy, dancing through the fog.

She spun away from the window, her heart pounding, and crept out of her room. Down the stairs, as silently as she could. And out the backdoor.

The fog billowed around her, damp and warm. She could feel the moisture on her skin as she stepped into the yard, her eyes adjusting to the moonlight.

Shadows flickered and tossed beneath the fog swirls. The trees rose up at the back of the yard like dark giants. A curtain of fog fell between the two yards, hiding the fence that separated Jenny's house from Mrs. Warsaw's.

Jenny heard another howl, distant now. She

turned, trying to figure out its direction. Eager to follow it.

She heard laughter, a high, boyish giggle. Cold laughter. Cruel.

"Sean — is that you?" she called. "Sean?" Silence.

The dark trees shivered in a hot gust of wind. Shadows bent and tossed.

What am I doing out here? she asked herself.

Solving the mystery, came the answer.

Solving the mystery so no one can accuse you of being crazy.

Solving the mystery so you never have to return to that hospital.

Another shrill laugh. Right behind her?

She whirled around. Stared into the fog. Saw only flickering shadows.

"Sean? Are you out here? Answer me — please!"

The next giggle made her jump. So close. So close it could be coming from her own mouth. Inside her own head.

No!

No, I'm *not* imagining it!

No. It's real. It's real laughter.

The blood pounded at her temples. Despite the heat, Jenny felt chills.

She took a step toward the Warsaws' yard. Then another.

"Sean? Are you laughing? Are you out here?"

And then Jenny uttered a startled gasp as she heard thudding footsteps.

She felt hot breath on the back of her neck — as two strong hands shoved her hard from behind.

Chapter 20

Jenny landed hard on her elbows and knees.

With a frightened cry, she spun around and stared up at the enormous creature, panting excitedly beside her.

"Killer!" she cried hoarsely. "What are you doing out here?"

The big German shepherd wagged his shaggy tail at the sound of his name. His sides moved in and out like bellows, and his tongue hung out between his jagged teeth.

"You're hot, huh?" Jenny asked, climbing to her knees.

The dog lumbered forward and licked Jenny's face, nearly toppling her over again.

"Killer, you scared me to death," Jenny told the dog, scratching his collar. She shoved him away gently and pulled herself to her feet. "Are you being a good watchdog?"

The dog panted loudly in reply.

"Did you see a boy out here, Killer?" Jenny demanded, letting her eyes wander around the yard.

She pushed her hair back off her face. It felt so wet. She wiped the sweat off her forehead with the back of one hand.

Killer lumbered toward the fence, sniffing the ground, his tail straight up behind him. She watched him until he disappeared behind the curtain of fog.

Jenny turned back toward her house.

I've lost him, she thought, disappointed. No sign of the blond-haired boy. Whoever it was, he's gone now.

And then she heard the shrill laughter, so close, so close to her . . . so cold and ugly.

"Who's there?" Jenny cried. "Who?"

No one there.

"Jenny?" a familiar voice shouted. "Jenny? Come here!"

Her mother called to her from the back-door.

The kitchen light flashed on as Jenny made her way into the house. Mrs. Jeffers stood in her bathrobe, her face lined with worry, her eyes still half-closed with sleep, her hands pressed tightly at her waist.

"Mom, I . . . uh . . ." Jenny started.

"What on earth?" Mrs. Jeffers exclaimed.

"What were you doing out there, Jen? It's nearly two in the morning."

"Well . . ." Jenny took a deep breath. She swallowed hard, tried to slow her pounding heart.

"Look at you!" her mother cried. "You're soaked! You're dripping wet. What were you doing out there?"

Jenny pushed back her hair again. She suddenly felt weak. Exhausted. "I heard those howls again," she told her mother. "I saw a boy. A blond boy. I thought it was — "

"You got dressed and chased after him?" Mrs. Jeffers demanded.

"I — I stayed dressed," Jenny confessed. "I had to find out — "

Mrs. Jeffers' jaw twitched. "We'll have to have a talk in the morning," she said softly. "A serious talk, Jen." She let out a long sigh.

"But, Mom — "

"I can't let you baby-sit next door anymore," her mother continued, tensely shoving her hands into the robe pockets. "It hasn't been good for you. These things you're seeing. These voices and things — "

Jenny let out a shriek. "Claire *told* you?" she cried.

Mrs. Jeffers nodded grimly. "She called me this afternoon. She told me . . . about you."

Jenny balled her hands into tight fists. "She *promised* me! She promised me she wouldn't tell!" she raged.

"Jen — she's your friend. She's worried about you," Mrs. Jeffers replied softly, her jaw clenching and unclenching again. "She did what she thought was best for you."

Jenny paced furiously back and forth. "I can't *believe* she called you!" she cried. She glared angrily at her mother. "Does *everyone* around here think I'm totally Looney Tunes? Even my best friend?"

"No one thinks you're sick again," Mrs. Jeffers replied, speaking carefully. "But you know yourself that you're supposed to avoid strain. You're not supposed to stress yourself out." She sighed. "We'll call Dr. Simonson in the morning. I'm sure that she will want to talk — "

Jenny stopped pacing. She locked her eyes on her mother. "Mom, I'm going back to Mrs. Warsaw's," she said firmly. "I don't care what you say. I'm not crazy. I'm not imagining anything."

"Jen — it's late," her mother started. "And you've gotten yourself worked up into a state. In the morning — "

"Mom, Mrs. Warsaw needs me," Jenny insisted, speaking slowly, softly. "I'm going back there to baby-sit. One more time. One more time, Mom. And I'm going to find out what's going on over there. So that no one can call me crazy again."

"Jenny, you look tired," Mrs. Warsaw said. She stood in her kitchen, loading plastic containers of food into two large brown shopping bags.

Jenny sighed. "I didn't get much sleep last night." She picked up a container labeled SOUP and handed it to Mrs. Warsaw.

"I kept hearing the strangest howls all night," Jenny continued. "Out in back. Did you hear them, too?"

Mrs. Warsaw shook her head. Her tight ringlets bounced around her face. "I'm a very heavy sleeper," she replied. "The house could fall in, and I wouldn't hear it."

Jenny had hurried over after dinner. Her mother tried to convince her not to baby-sit. "I'll go in your place," Mrs. Jeffers offered.

"I'll be okay, Mom," Jenny assured her. "Mrs. Warsaw said she's only staying at her sister's for a short while." Jenny had forced a smile. She squeezed her mother's hand. "Besides, you're right next door. What can happen?"

Now she helped Mrs. Warsaw load the food

bags into the backseat of her car. "Where are the kids?" she asked.

Mrs. Warsaw brushed a mosquito off her chubby arm. "Upstairs. In Sean's room, I think. They were playing a board game last time I checked."

Jenny followed Mrs. Warsaw back to the house. The sun was setting behind the trees. A white half-moon hovered low in the graying sky.

Mrs. Warsaw pulled her car keys from her bag. She hoisted the bag on her shoulder and headed out the door. "Don't let Meredith stay up too late," she instructed. "She looked a little pale to me today."

Jenny nodded. "No problem." The screen door slammed behind Mrs. Warsaw. Jenny glanced quickly around the kitchen.

Her eyes stopped at the sink. She felt a chill as she remembered the grinding roar of the garbage disposal, the powerful, invisible force that pushed her hand into the drain.

Swallowing hard, she forced herself to turn away from the sink. Her heart pounding, she ran from the kitchen.

She found the three kids in the twins' room. They were seated on the floor around a game board. Cards and dice and scorecards were scattered around the board.

Both boys were barefoot. They both wore baggy blue shorts without shirts.

They're both so pale and skinny, Jenny thought. I can practically see their ribs.

Meredith was already dressed for bed, in an enormous white T-shirt that came down to her ankles.

"Hey, guys — what's up?' Jenny called cheerfully.

"We're playing Clue," Sean told her.

Meredith frowned up at Jenny. "I don't really *get* this game."

"It's kind of a hard game for you," Jenny replied.

"I'm helping her," Seth said.

Jenny lowered herself to the carpet and watched the game. The culprit turned out to be Colonel Mustard in the library with the candlestick.

Seth was the first to figure it out. Meredith shook her head unhappily. "How did you *do* that?" she asked her brother. "I still don't get it."

Jenny started to relax. The kids seemed to be in very good moods, less tense than usual. She joined in the next game. They played quietly, without any arguing at all.

After a second game, Jenny tucked

Meredith into bed. Then she helped the boys put the game away.

Seth kept staring at her, she noticed. He seemed to be watching her, studying her.

She followed them downstairs. They wanted to watch TV.

But Jenny decided she had to ask them some questions.

She made them sit side by side on the living room couch. Then she stood in front of them, her arms crossed over her chest.

"Did we do something wrong?" Sean asked innocently.

"I just want to ask you about something," Jenny replied. She paused, thinking hard, trying to decide where to begin.

The boys exchanged glances. Sean scratched his bare chest.

"Last night, I heard strange noises outside," Jenny began. "And I looked out my window and saw a boy running across the backyard."

She turned to Sean. "Was that *you* running outside after midnight last night?"

Sean's eyes widened. He glanced again at his brother. When he turned back to Jenny, he had a fretful expression on his face.

"Yes," he said softly, so softly Jenny could barely hear him. "It was me."

Chapter 21

Her arms still crossed tightly in front of her, Jenny stared down at Sean. She hadn't expected him to confess.

A grin spread over Seth's face. He giggled and poked Sean hard with his elbow.

Sean's solemn expression cracked, and he started to giggle, too. The boys slapped each other high fives.

Jenny stared at them in confusion. "You mean — ?" she stated.

"You're such a jerk!" Seth told his brother. They both giggled some more.

"It wasn't Sean. It was me!" Seth declared, laughing.

"Liar!" Sean cried, shoving his brother. "It was me! I go out every night and howl at the moon!"

They both tossed back their heads and started to howl at the top of their lungs.

"Ssshhh! Quiet! Stop it!" Jenny demanded angrily. "Meredith is trying to sleep — remember?"

Sean and Seth continued to giggle, very pleased with themselves.

"Ha-ha," Jenny said sarcastically. "You guys are a riot." She sighed angrily. "You didn't have to lie to me. I asked you a serious question."

Their grins faded. "Did you really see a boy in the backyard?" Seth demanded.

"Yes," Jenny replied quickly. "I mean . . . I'm *pretty* sure. I know I heard him laughing. And . . . and . . ."

"It was very foggy last night," Seth said.

"How do *you* know?" Jenny asked suspiciously.

"I woke up. I was very thirsty. I looked out my window. It was really creepy out. Kind of scary-looking."

For some reason, Seth's explanation made Sean laugh and shake his head.

Seth flashed his brother an angry glance, and Sean cut his laughter short.

"Can we make popcorn?" Sean asked.

Jenny raised her eyes to the mantel clock. "It's kind of late."

"We'll go to bed right after popcorn," Sean promised.

Jenny reluctantly agreed. She headed to the kitchen, thinking about what had just happened. The boys had treated my question about last night as a total joke, she realized. They didn't take me seriously for a moment.

But I did see a blond-haired boy running through the fog last night.

And if it wasn't Sean or Seth — who was it?

They didn't go to bed after popcorn, as promised. They begged to watch TV. When there wasn't anything on that they liked, they begged to play just one Super-Nintendo game.

Which turned into *two* games.

It was nearly eleven when Jenny finally tucked them into bed. She said good night, turned down their second requests for a glass of water, and returned to the living room.

She gazed uncertainly around the room. She picked up the game cartridges and stacked them beside the TV. Then she started to pace nervously back and forth.

So far, the evening had been peaceful. Even relaxing.

But Jenny knew that when the kids were tucked in their beds . . .

When the kids were tucked in and the house fell quiet . . .

That's when the eerie chill descended over the room. That's when the frightening whispers came.

As they did tonight.

As they did again tonight.

The horrifying, whispered threat. So close . . . so close to Jenny's ear.

The same tonight. But different. Much different.

"Jenny, you saw me."

She stopped pacing. Whirled around. Felt the sudden whiff of frigid air.

Her eyes swept the room.

But of course she saw no one.

"Who are you? What do you want?" she choked out.

"Jenny, you saw me last night," the voice repeated. So close. As if whispering in her ear. *"Now you have to die. Now you have to die TONIGHT!"*

Chapter 22

Jenny uttered a gasp as the cold swirled around her.

She felt the clammy touch of bone-hard fingers against her cheek.

"Noooooo!" A terrified howl burst from her throat.

She pulled back, away from the cold, invisible touch.

Stumbled against the coffee table. Struggled to keep from falling backwards over it.

The icy fingers slid over the back of her neck.

"Nooooooo!"

She ducked away. Spun toward the stairs. Started to run.

A damp chill, a wave of cold swept over her, holding her, pushing her back.

She heard laughter, as cold as the air.

"You die tonight, Jenny!"

She opened her mouth to scream again. But the sound choked in her throat.

The chill air rolled over her, washed against her, wave after wave.

She ducked her head, shut her eyes, and dove through the cold.

The stairs rose in front of her.

The cruel laughter followed close behind as she plunged into the stairwell.

The stairs tilted and swayed.

She grasped the iron banister. Pulled herself up, step by step.

She felt the cold at her back. Heard the laughter rising behind her.

Where can I go? she asked herself. *Where can I hide?*

She stumbled at the landing. Hit her knee hard on the top step.

The cold swept over her. Pushed her back into the stairwell.

A choking, thick cold that took her breath away.

She sucked in a mouthful of air. It tasted sour.

Her eyes darted over the narrow hall-way.

Where to run? Where to hide?

Into the bathroom across from the twins' room.

She grabbed frantically for the door. Slammed it hard behind her.

Locked it with a trembling hand.

Stood in the dark for a long moment. Not breathing. Not moving.

Listening. Listening for the laughter. For the whispery voice.

Her heart thudding, making her chest ache. Flashing streaks of white light blazing in her eyes. She blinked. Blinked again.

Am I safe here in the darkness?

Have I shut the voice out? Have I shut the owner of the clammy fingers out in the hall?

Silence. Such a heavy silence.

She fumbled for the light switch. Clicked on the ceiling light. It flickered on.

So bright.

She waited for her eyes to adjust.

Listened. Listened.

Silence still.

Jenny raised her eyes to the medicine chest mirror.

She gasped when she saw the reflection.

A face stared back at her.

Not her face.

Sean's face.

Chapter 23

Jenny uttered a startled cry.

She spun around. "How — how did you get in here?" she stammered.

No one there.

Her eyes bulged in disbelief.

She turned back to the mirror.

He smiled out at her in the glass.

She spun back toward the door.

Not there.

No one there but her.

She stood alone in the tiny bathroom.

"Noooo!" A moan of horror burst from her lips.

The pale face grinned gleefully at her from the mirror.

"Are you — are you Sean?" she choked out.

The face in the mirror shook his head no. His grin didn't fade. His eyes gleamed with pleasure.

"You're *Seth*?" Jenny demanded.

His grin widened as he nodded yes.

"Oh." Her entire body convulsed in a tremor of shock.

"Seth — where are you? Seth?"

Jenny spun around again.

Not there. Not standing behind her.

She pulled back the shower curtain.

Not hiding in the tub.

Not in the room. Not there.

But grinning out at her from the mirror.

"Seth — please — " she started.

His grin faded quickly. His eyes narrowed cruelly. His expression hardened until Jenny barely recognized him.

"Jenny — you die TONIGHT!" Seth whispered from the mirror.

Chapter 24

The cold rose up from the bathroom floor.

In the mirror, Seth's leering face began to glow. Brighter. Brighter. Until his whole head gleamed like gold.

"Jenny — you die TONIGHT!"

"It was you!" Jenny shrieked in a shrill voice that tore out of her throbbing chest. "Seth — it was you! But — why?"

"The baby-sitter has to die!" the glowing reflection cried.

"No!" Jenny shrieked. "No!"

The boy's face sneered at her from inside the glass.

"No! No!" She chanted without hearing herself.

With a gasp of terror, of anger, of panic, she grabbed up the heavy china flower vase that rested beside the sink.

Tilted the dried flowers out onto the vanity counter.

Pulled back her arm.

And let out a defiant cry as she heaved the vase at the leering face in the mirror.

The face appeared to crack as the mirror shattered.

Jenny gaped in horror, watching the vase tumble to the floor. Watching the face in the mirror appear to split apart.

Sections of mirror fell away.

Then the whole mirror toppled out of its frame.

Shards of glass flew.

Jenny reached out to shield herself.

And a jagged piece of mirror scraped over her open hand.

She didn't feel it at first.

Then a line of pain shot up her arm. And she stared in surprise as the bright red blood spurted up from the deep cut in her hand and flowed over her wrist.

"Ohhh." She grabbed at her wrist. Watched the blood smear over her other hand.

Watched it drip, drip, drip to the floor. A bright red rivulet, so warm.

"Jenny — ?"

A voice behind her.

Someone else in the room.

"Jenny — ?"

Holding her throbbing hand, feeling the warm blood flow down her arm, Jenny turned.

"Mrs. Warsaw!"

The woman filled the doorway, her mouth open in shock, her eyes lowered to the flowing, dripping blood. "Jenny — what have you done?" she cried. "How — ?"

"I — I — " Jenny sputtered. She raised her hand to point to the medicine chest, and the blood dripped down the front of her T-shirt.

"What have you done?" Mrs. Warsaw murmured again. She slid past Jenny, into the room, careful to step around the widening puddle of blood on the white tile floor.

"I — I — " Jenny still couldn't find the words.

Mrs. Warsaw frantically began pulling up tissues from the dispenser on the counter. Broken glass crunched beneath her shoes.

She jammed a thick wad of tissues against the cut on Jenny's hand. "Let's get you home. Quick. Let's get you home."

"Th-thank you," Jenny finally managed to say. The words sounded odd. Out of place. Meaningless. She didn't know what else to say.

They started out the door. Jenny glanced down at the trail of blood she was leaving.

"Wait." Mrs. Warsaw stopped, turned. She grabbed a green bath towel off the rack. She wrapped it tightly around Jenny's wrist. "Hold it. Hold it in place," she instructed. "We've got to stop that bleeding."

Jenny nodded. She struggled to hold the towel in place. Her legs felt rubbery and weak as she followed Mrs. Warsaw into the hall.

Down the stairs.

Jenny let out a moan of pain. Mrs. Warsaw wrapped a heavy arm around her waist and guided her out the backdoor. Into a warm, starless night.

"How did you do that?" Mrs. Warsaw murmured as they hurried toward Jenny's house. "How did you ever do it?"

Jenny's mom appeared at the backdoor. The light came on. Then Jenny saw her mother running barefoot across the yard, running to meet them.

"What happened? What happened?" Mrs. Jeffers cried. She gasped as she drew closer. "Oh! So much blood!"

"We've got to get a doctor," Mrs. Warsaw urged. "We've got to stop the bleeding."

"Just a cut," Jenny managed to tell her mother. "Not as bad as it looks. Really."

"But what happened?" Mrs. Jeffers demanded, helping guide Jenny into the house.

"The mirror broke," Mrs. Warsaw told her. "Glass all over."

"The twins," Jenny murmured, trying to clear her head, trying to explain to them.

"What?" Mrs. Warsaw's face filled with confusion.

"Sean and Seth," Jenny said. "I saw Seth in the yard at night. And then in the mirror, and — "

"Who?" Mrs. Warsaw demanded.

Mrs. Jeffers stared at Jenny, her features tight with concern.

"Your twins," Jenny repeated. "I knew there was something strange about the twins. But — I just couldn't figure it out. Until . . . until . . ."

"Oh, child!" Mrs. Warsaw sighed, her eyes brimming with tears. "Oh, child. Oh, child."

"Something strange about the twins," Jenny insisted.

Mrs. Warsaw placed a tender hand on Jenny's trembling shoulder. "Oh, child," she repeated. "Oh, Jenny. You poor thing. I don't *have* twins!"

Chapter 25

Jenny stared down at her bandaged hand. It made her think of mummies.

That's what I'll be, she thought glumly, letting a tear roll down her cheek. That's what I'll be if I have to go back to the hospital. A mummy. Locked tightly away.

A loud sob escaped her throat. But she forced back the tears that threatened to fall.

Her mother had cleaned the cut and carefully bandaged it. It hadn't been as deep as it seemed. It wouldn't require stitches.

Mrs. Jeffers took Jenny up to her bedroom and told her to lie down and rest. A few seconds later, Jenny overheard her mother on the phone. She had called Dr. Simonson. She was leaving a message about Jenny on her answering machine.

Mom thinks I'm crazy, Jenny told herself.

I *am* crazy!

No twins. No twins.

The words repeated in her mind like a sorrowful chant.

Mrs. Warsaw doesn't have twins. She only has Sean and Meredith.

That means I imagined Seth, Jenny told herself. That means I imagined a boy who looks just like Sean.

But — wait.

Sean talked to Seth, too.

And Meredith talked to Seth.

Both kids played ball with Seth. Seth and Sean played video games together all the time.

So how could I have made him up? Jenny asked herself. How could Seth exist only in my mind?

She shut her eyes and pressed both hands against her throbbing temples. So confused . . . I'm so totally confused.

She could hear her mother down in the kitchen, talking to Mrs. Warsaw.

They're talking about me, Jenny knew. They're talking about how crazy I am, how I saw a boy that doesn't exist.

Jenny climbed to her feet. She crept out of the room, to the stairway. She stopped halfway down, listening to the conversation in the kitchen.

"The doctor will know what's best," Mrs.

Jeffers was saying. "I just can't believe it's
. . . happening to Jenny again."

Mrs. Warsaw muttered a reply. Jenny
couldn't hear it.

Jenny sat down on the step and rested her
head against the wooden banister.

After a few seconds, she heard Mrs.
Warsaw continue. "We almost didn't buy the
house. You know. Because of the stories."

"Stories?" Jenny heard her mother ask.

"About the boy," Mrs. Warsaw explained.
"The boy who was murdered in the house. By
his baby-sitter. When the real estate agent told
us, I wasn't sure I wanted to live here."

A long silence.

Jenny lifted her head. Listened hard, her
mind spinning.

"Oh, how horrible!" her mother exclaimed
to Mrs. Warsaw. "Maybe Jenny heard the
story about the murdered boy. Maybe it
stayed buried in her mind somehow. And
when she started going to your house to baby-
sit . . ."

"The boy came to life in Jenny's mind," Mrs.
Warsaw finished the sentence for Jenny's
mother.

"No!" Jenny murmured out loud. "No. I
didn't imagine Seth. I'm not crazy! I'm not!"

"I'm taking Sean and Meredith to my sister's," she heard Mrs. Warsaw announce.

"When?" Mrs. Jeffers asked.

"Right now. I want to spend the night with my sister. I might stay for a day or two." A pause. And then Mrs. Warsaw added, "I hope everything is all right. With Jenny."

"I hope so, too," Jenny's mother replied uncertainly.

I'm *not* crazy! Jenny thought, jumping to her feet. I'm *not* going back to the hospital! Never!

She heard the backdoor slam. Heard her mother making her way to the stairs. Jenny turned and ran back to her room.

She sat down in the dark on the edge of the bed. Then she stood up and started to pace, her arms crossed in front of her.

A boy was murdered, she thought. A boy was murdered in Mrs. Warsaw's house. Murdered by his baby-sitter.

"Jenny? Are you okay?" Mrs. Jeffers stepped into the room. "What are you doing?" She clicked on the ceiling light.

"Just thinking," Jenny replied.

Mrs. Jeffers crossed the room quickly and hugged Jenny. "You'll be okay. I know you will. Get undressed, okay? Get some sleep. Tomorrow morning we'll . . ." Her voice trailed off.

"We'll go see Dr. Simonson," Jenny finished the thought for her.

"That little boy you saw — " Mrs. Jeffers started.

"He was *there*, Mom!" Jenny cried heatedly. "You've got to believe me. I didn't make him up! He was there!"

Her mother sighed. "Please get some sleep, Jenny. I know you'll feel a lot better after we see the doctor."

For several minutes after her mother left the room, Jenny continued to pace back and forth, thinking hard, thinking about Seth, about how sweet he had seemed. And then she remembered his cruel, hard face in the bathroom mirror. His taunting laugh. His threats.

"The baby-sitter has to die!" Seth had said. So angrily. So bitterly.

I didn't make it up, Jenny told herself for the hundredth time. I didn't make Seth up.

She heard voices in the backyard. Peering out the window, she saw Mrs. Warsaw load the two kids into the backseat of her car. Sean and Meredith were in pajamas. Meredith clutched a small brown teddy bear.

A few seconds later, the headlights flashed on, and the car backed down the driveway and rolled off into the night.

Jenny sighed.

Two kids. Just two kids.

She started to turn away — but a movement in the upstairs window of the Warsaws' house caught her eye.

Something moved in the attic window next door.

Jenny squinted into the moonlight.

A face. A face in the attic window.

Jenny recognized it. The girl. The sad-eyed girl.

She was staring back at Jenny. And again her lips moved in the same silent plea: "Help me. Help me."

Am I imagining her, too? Jenny wondered. Is she only in my mind?

She had to find out.

"Help me," the girl pleaded, her face pressed against the glass. "Help me."

"Okay," Jenny said out loud. "I'll help you. I'm coming over there. Right now."

Chapter 26

She paused at the bottom of the stairs, making sure her mother hadn't heard. Then she slipped out the front door, carefully closing the screen door behind her.

As she silently made her way around to the back, Jenny gazed up at the Warsaws' attic window. The moon had sunk behind heavy clouds. Darkness covered the window now.

I'm coming, Jenny thought, searching for the sad-eyed girl. I'm coming to let you out. Whoever you are.

She stumbled over Sean's bike in the drive-way, but caught her balance. Her heart pounded as she stepped up to the Warsaws' backdoor.

So dark. Without the moon shining down, the house hovered in total blackness, like a dark, silent creature waiting to swallow her up.

Jenny tried the backdoor. It pushed open easily. In all the confusion, Mrs. Warsaw had left it unlocked. Taking a deep breath, Jenny slipped into the house.

Past the cluttered kitchen. The empty popcorn bowls from earlier that night still strewn on the counter. Mrs. Warsaw hadn't bothered to clean up. She must have been really eager to get back to her sister's, Jenny realized.

Her sneakers squeaked on the linoleum as she crossed the kitchen and made her way into the living room. Her heart thudded in her chest. Her skin began to tingle.

She climbed the stairs slowly, pulling herself up one step at a time. She listened hard, alert to every sound, every creak of the stairs, every sigh of the house.

She stopped at the second-floor landing. The hallway was too dark to see anything. The door to the attic was down at the other end.

Jenny fumbled along the wall. Found the light switch. Clicked on the yellow ceiling light.

The narrow hall stretched before her. Silent. The air so hot and stuffy.

She glanced at the boys' room. No. At *Sean's* room. She stepped into the doorway, examined the bunk bed against the wall. The covers were pulled back only on the bottom bunk. Sean's bed. The blanket on the top bunk was smooth and unruffled.

No twins. No twins.

Only Sean in this room.

But hadn't she seen him sleeping up there?

Hadn't she brought them both glasses of water? Hadn't she stood in this doorway, arguing with them both about their bedtime?

With a sigh, Jenny spun away. Crossed the hall. Stepped up to the attic door.

She listened for the footsteps overhead.

Silence.

She grabbed the doorknob. Started to turn it.

She screamed as cold, bony fingers wrapped around her hand.

Chapter 27

"Jenny — don't!" A harsh whisper in her ear.

Jenny turned. "Seth — !" she cried. "You're still here!"

His hand felt so clammy against hers.

"Don't let her out," he pleaded. "Please, Jenny — don't let her hurt me again." Seth let go of Jenny's hand. He lowered his head sadly.

"Seth — you — you're real!" Jenny stammered.

She had to make sure. She reached out both hands and grabbed his tiny shoulders. "You're alive!" Jenny declared.

He shook his head. His shoulders trembled beneath her hands. "No, I'm not," he whispered. "I'm not alive."

"Huh?" Jenny jerked back her hands.

"I'm dead, Jenny," Seth murmured, his head still lowered. "I'm dead — because *she* killed me!" He pointed to the attic door.

"But Seth — " Jenny started.

To her surprise, he threw his arms around her waist and held on to her tightly, burying his face in her T-shirt.

She could feel his whole body shaking. She felt hot tears dampen the front of her shirt. "Seth — " she whispered.

"You've been so nice to me," he said in a tiny voice, holding on to her tightly. "I know I was mean to you. But I couldn't help myself. I was so mixed up, Jenny. Because she . . . my baby-sitter . . . she killed me. Killed me for no reason."

A wave of sorrow swept over Jenny. She sifted her hands through his blond hair. So fine and light she could barely feel it.

"Don't let her out, Jenny. She has to stay locked up there. Please don't open the door," Seth pleaded softly, pressing his face against her waist.

"Seth, I don't know — " Jenny started uncertainly. "That girl looks so sad. She — "

"She killed me!" Seth cried. "Jenny — please. You've been so nice. You're the only one who was nice to me. I've lived in this house for so long and — "

"The other kids — " Jenny interrupted.

"Sean and Meredith. They knew you were here. They knew you were a ghost, right, Seth? They talked with you. They played with you."

Seth nodded. "I like them. They were nice to me, too. That's why I made myself look like Sean. I really wanted to be his twin, Jenny. I really wanted to have Sean for a brother."

That's so sad, Jenny thought, feeling tears brim in her eyes. "And they never told their mother about you?" Jenny asked softly.

"They liked me," Seth replied. "They wouldn't tell on me. They kept the secret because they liked me."

"And the howls at night?" Jenny demanded. "The vandalism around the neighborhood? The boy I saw running through my backyard?"

"It was me," Seth confessed, lowering his eyes. "Sometimes I couldn't help myself. Sometimes I had to get out of this house. Sometimes I felt trapped in here. I had to break free."

"You said you were going to kill me," Jenny accused, narrowing her eyes at him, forcing him to look up at her. "You tried to scare me, Seth. You tried to hurt me."

His chest heaved as he let out a sob. "I was so mixed up, Jenny. I didn't really want to hurt you. Sometimes I just couldn't help myself."

Ugly pictures flashed into Jenny's mind.
She remembered the cake knife that nearly
plunged through her chest. She remembered
the roaring garbage disposal, the strong force
pushing her hand down into the drain.

She grabbed the door handle.

"No, Jenny!" Seth insisted, his eyes grow-
ing wide with fear.

She didn't remove her hand. "Seth, I have
to know the truth," she said softly.

"Please." Again, Seth covered her hand
with his. "She's bad, Jenny. She's really bad."

"I have to talk to her," Jenny said, clenching
her jaw. "I have to see her."

"The door is locked," Seth told her shrilly.
"You can't open it. You can't!"

"It's an old door," Jenny replied. "I can pull
it open."

"No! *I won't let you!*" he shrieked, his face
wild with fear.

Jenny turned the doorknob. And tugged.

The lock gave easily. The door swung open
with startling force.

The dark-haired girl burst out, in a long,
gray sweater over a black skirt, a triumphant
smile on her face.

The smile faded as she gazed at Seth.

And then her eyes glowed red and her mouth twisted in an ugly frown as she turned to Jenny.

"Noooo! Oh no!" Seth screamed. "She killed me, Jenny — and now she's going to kill *you*!"

Chapter 28

The girl took a lurching step toward Jenny, her pale face twisted in fury. Her dark hair rose up around her head. Her eyes burned like flames.

"Monica — please!" Seth shrieked, backing away. "I warned you, Jenny! I warned you!"

Jenny stumbled back. Hit the wall. "I — I just wanted to help you, Monica," she choked out.

"At last!" the girl cried hoarsely. "At last! At last! After so many years!"

She spun around. Turned her scarlet glare on Seth.

"She killed me, Jenny! She killed me!" Seth cried, his eyes wide with horror.

"Liar!" Monica seethed. "Liar! You killed *me*! You killed *me*, Seth!"

Seth's eyes narrowed. His expression turned hard. He didn't reply.

"You killed me!" Monica repeated, advancing on him. "Locked me in the attic. And then you were so joyful . . . so excited . . . so thrilled by your triumph — you fell down the stairs. You fell and died. What a horrible accident, Seth. A horrible accident took your life — *after* you took mine!"

"Don't listen to her," Seth instructed Jenny. "She'll say anything. We have to lock her back up. We *have* to — before she kills again!"

"For ten years, I've been locked up in that attic," Monica continued, explaining to Jenny. "Unable to rest. Unable to find any peace. Listening to Seth. Listening to him terrify the people who lived in this house."

"Liar!" Seth cried furiously. "People like me. People feel sorry for me — because you killed me. Sean and Meredith *liked* me. They kept my secret because they *liked* me!"

Monica narrowed her dark eyes at Seth. "They kept your secret because you threatened them," she accused. "You hurt them. You said you'd *kill* them if they ever told anyone the truth about you."

Her entire body trembling in fear, Jenny pressed her back against the wall, watching the two ghostly figures rage at each other.

Which one should I believe? Jenny asked herself.

Which one is telling the truth?

She didn't have time to decide.

Monica turned on her, her eyes gleaming red like those of a wild creature. "Thank you for rescuing me, Jenny," she snarled. "I'm really sorry for what I have to do now."

Her eyes glowed even brighter as she advanced on Jenny. Panting excitedly, her hands balled into tight fists, she loomed over Jenny.

"See? I warned you!" Seth called. "I warned you!"

With a soft grunt, Monica grabbed Jenny around the waist — and lifted her easily off the floor.

"Put me down!" Jenny screamed, flailing her arms. "Put me down!"

Ignoring Jenny's terrified pleas, Monica carried her to the stairway.

Lifted her higher.

Jenny thrashed her legs, tried to kick free.

But Monica gripped her with inhuman strength.

She's going to throw me down the stairs! Jenny realized.

"I warned you, Jenny! I warned you!" Seth called from the hallway.

Chapter 29

Jenny shut her eyes.

Every muscle in her body locked.

She couldn't breathe. She couldn't move.

She waited helplessly for Monica to heave her down, waited for the thud of impact. Waited for the pain to shoot through her body.

To her surprise, Monica set her down gently on her feet.

Jenny's eyes shot open.

Monica had placed her on the top step.

"I want you out of the way," the ghostly girl murmured. "I want you to be safe." She brushed her cheek against Jenny's. "Thank you, Jenny," she whispered. "I'll never forget you."

And, then, before Jenny could react, before Jenny could utter a word, Monica flung herself at Seth.

As Monica tackled him to the floor, Seth

uttered a snarl of rage. Leaning into the hall, Jenny saw his features transform.

The light blond hair appeared to be sucked inside his skull as his head grew and changed shape. His pale skin darkened to a sickening green. Ugly brown sores splotched his bald skull. And he opened his mouth wide to reveal jagged rows of yellow, pointed teeth.

He slashed at Monica with hair-covered claws.

She held on to him tightly, burying her teeth in his neck.

Roaring, biting, thrashing, they wrestled on the floor.

Then, still battling, they were on their feet.

Struggling. Groaning. Howling like wolves. Tangled in each other. Spinning in a furious dance of hatred.

Spinning. Spinning.

Until a whirlwind of black smoke spun around them.

Faster and faster, a dark funnel cloud, swirling around the two ghosts, blanketing them from Jenny's view.

Thick, black smoke, whipping round and around, whistling as it spun, whistling over the angry howls and grunts of pain.

A final hoarse cry.

From Seth? From Monica?

The smoke settled slowly, sinking, sinking into the carpet.

The hallway stood empty.

Empty and silent.

Jenny leaned against the wall, her legs trembling, her heart pounding. She watched the dark smoke lower over the carpet, like a shadow.

And then it was gone.

And the ghosts had vanished with it.

I'm alone now, Jenny thought, letting out a long *whoosh* of air. I'm all alone now.

But, no.

She turned when she heard the voices below her. Voices calling her name.

Lights flashed on downstairs. Mrs. Jeffers peered up the stairs at Jenny. "Huh? You're here?"

Cal appeared beside her mother. He ran up the stairs, put an arm gently around Jenny's shoulder.

"Jenny — what are you *doing* here?" her mother demanded shrilly, her voice revealing her alarm.

"I . . . uh . . . had to see something," Jenny muttered.

"I was so worried," Mrs. Jeffers declared. "I called Cal. I thought maybe you went over there. But . . ."

Cal sniffed the air. "I smell smoke," he said.

"No. It's okay," Jenny assured him. She leaned against him, let him guide her down the steps.

"We searched everywhere," Jenny's mom continued. "Then Cal and I saw a light on over here, and — "

When she reached the bottom of the stairs, Jenny threw her arms around her mother's shoulders and held her close. "I'm okay now, Mom," she told her softly. "Really. I'm okay now. You don't have to worry about me anymore. I've been through a lot. And now I know I'm really strong."

Mrs. Jeffers stared hard at Jenny, as if trying to decide if her words were true. "I — I'm very glad," she finally managed to stammer.

With an arm around each of their waists, Jenny led the way out of the Warsaws' house. The half-moon had found its way out from behind the clouds. The back lawn glistened as if filled with thousands of tiny diamonds.

"You never have to baby-sit again," Mrs. Jeffers told Jenny. "Really. I mean it. No more baby-sitting."

Jenny smiled. "That's okay, Mom," she replied brightly. "I might want to baby-sit again someday. It's a lot more exciting than you think."

About the Author

R.L. STINE is the author of more than three dozen mysteries for young people, all of which have been best-sellers. Recent Scholastic horror titles include *Halloween Night II*, *I Saw You That Night!*, *Call Waiting*, and *The Dead Girlfriend*.

In addition, he is the author of two popular monthly series: *Goosebumps* and *Fear Street*.

Bob lives in New York City with his wife, Jane, and fifteen-year-old son, Matt.

THRILLERS

D.E. Athkins
- ☐ MC45246-0 Mirror, Mirror — $3.25
- ☐ MC45349-1 The Ripper — $3.25
- ☐ MC44941-9 Sister Dearest — $2.95

A. Bates
- ☐ MC45829-9 The Dead Game — $3.25
- ☐ MC43291-5 Final Exam — $3.25
- ☐ MC44582-0 Mother's Helper — $3.50
- ☐ MC44238-4 Party Line — $3.25

Caroline B. Cooney
- ☐ MC44316-X The Cheerleader — $3.25
- ☐ MC41641-3 The Fire — $3.25
- ☐ MC43806-9 The Fog — $3.25
- ☐ MC45681-4 Freeze Tag — $3.25
- ☐ MC45402-1 The Perfume — $3.25
- ☐ MC44884-6 The Return of the Vampire — $2.95
- ☐ MC41640-5 The Snow — $3.25
- ☐ MC45680-6 The Stranger — $3.50
- ☐ MC45682-2 The Vampire's Promise — $3.50

Richie Tankersley Cusick
- ☐ MC43115-3 April Fools — $3.25
- ☐ MC43203-6 The Lifeguard — $3.25
- ☐ MC43114-5 Teacher's Pet — $3.25
- ☐ MC44235-X Trick or Treat — $3.25

Carol Ellis
- ☐ MC46411-6 Camp Fear — $3.25
- ☐ MC44768-8 My Secret Admirer — $3.25
- ☐ MC47101-5 Silent Witness — $3.25
- ☐ MC46044-7 The Stepdaughter — $3.25
- ☐ MC44916-8 The Window — $2.95

Lael Littke
- ☐ MC44237-6 Prom Dress — $3.25

Jane McFann
- ☐ MC46690-9 Be Mine — $3.25

Christopher Pike
- ☐ MC43014-9 Slumber Party — $3.50
- ☐ MC44256-2 Weekend — $3.50

Edited by T. Pines
- ☐ MC45256-8 Thirteen — $3.50

Sinclair Smith
- ☐ MC45063-8 The Waitress — $2.95

Barbara Steiner
- ☐ MC46425-6 The Phantom — $3.50

Robert Westall
- ☐ MC41693-6 Ghost Abbey — $3.25
- ☐ MC43761-5 The Promise — $3.25
- ☐ MC45176-6 Yaxley's Cat — $3.25

Available wherever you buy books, or use this order form.

Scholastic Inc., P.O. Box 7502, 2931 East McCarty Street, Jefferson City, MO 65102

Please send me the books I have checked above. I am enclosing $_____ (please add $2.00 to cover shipping and handling). Send check or money order — no cash or C.O.D.s please.

Name _____ Age _____

Address_____

City_____ State/Zip_____

Please allow four to six weeks for delivery. Offer good in the U.S. only. Sorry, mail orders are not available to residents of Canada. Prices subject to change.

T294

High on a hill,
trapped in the shadows,
something inside a dark house
is waiting...and watching.

THE HOUSE ON CHERRY STREET

A three-book series
by Rodman Philbrick and Lynn Harnett

Terror has a new home—and the children
are the only ones who sense it—from the
blasts of icy air in the driveway, to the windows
that shut like guillotines. Can Jason and Sally
stop the evil that lives in the dark?

HCS1194